OLIVE BRANCHES DON'T GROW ON TREES

GRACE MATTIOLI

Library of Congress Cataloging-in-Publication Data

Mattioli, Grace, 1965-

Olive Branches Don't Grow On Trees/ Grace Mattioli.

p. cm.

1. Families-Fiction 2.New Jersey-Fiction 3.Italian Americans-Fiction 4.Peace-Fiction

I. Title   PS3556.R352   813.54

ISBN: 978-0-9905751-0-8

DEDICATION

For my mom, who told me to save everything I write

And for my brother Vincent,
who told me I have a perfect sense of humor.

CHAPTER 1
THE SOUND OF NOISE

Silvia Greco knew that the silence would not last. There wasn't enough silence in her world, and there was definitely not enough of it since she had moved into her father's house in New Jersey. She knew that her father, Frank, had taken a brief break from his current project of searching for a lost frying pan, and that he would be resuming his search any second with the clattering of pots and pans and slamming of cabinet doors. In the very short meantime, she enjoyed the sound of nothing as she sat waiting for her coffee to finish brewing as if it was all she had left in the world.

She sat at a square wooden kitchen table that took over the entire room. It looked good from a distance, but upon closer inspection revealed several nicks and scratches that had given it a memory of its own– a bad one. The table was bare except for an economy sized bottle of TUMS displayed in the middle like a centerpiece. She sat on a chair that was almost too big for her little body. A big girl misplaced inside a little girl's body, she had a big voice, a big laugh, a big stride, a big Romanesque nose that sat proud beneath her big brown eyes. Her big head of hair was currently chopped in some crude style of uneven lengths, the color orange on the top and black at the bottom. Her hair style wasn't intended to be any sort of radical statement. It was just an expression of her current state of apathy. So was her attire– a paint covered T-shirt and worn out Levi jeans that hung on her as if they were five sizes too big. She usually dressed in bright bold sixties styled clothing that showed her off to the world as a happy, animated, free spirit. Her hair was usually evenly colored and stylized to perfection. But even with her grungy clothes and her chopped hair, she was pretty. And her big nose seemed to add to her prettiness in a way. Angie, her older sister, urged her to get her big nose made smaller with simple surgery, but Silvia refused to do such a thing, as if in doing so, she would be rejecting her Grandma Tucci, who had the same big nose and whom she loved fiercely.

Her father's nose was in perfect proportion to the rest of his face, which resembled that of an aged Marlon Brando. Despite a life time of working too hard, sleeping too little, drinking too much and smoking for the better half of his life, he still looked good. He had all of his hair and could sweep it from side to side depending on his mood. His physique looked as if he worked out at a gym on a regular basis, but he had never set foot in one. The slight limp he developed from being maimed in a motorcycle accident in his teen years was barely perceptible through his gargantuan personality. This was also the case with his slovenly attire of mismatched outfits and shirts buttoned unevenly with one side hanging down further than the other.

He had returned from the bathroom and wasted no time getting on with his project with a renewed sense of urgency. He gallivanted around the kitchen as if he was keeping beat to a polka song, searching for the lost pan while drinking and cooking something that smelled like an odd mixture of garlic and garbage left out in the rain. Silvia got up to get her coffee, careful not to get in her father's way. As she poured some milk into her coffee, the container slid out of her hand. It was greasy. She imagined that Frank had previously touched it with his olive oiled hands.

"I knew you were going to do that," said Frank who was suddenly standing over her shoulder. She wanted to say something like "Well maybe I wouldn't have spilled it if you didn't get your greasy hands all over it." She said nothing. She just cleaned up the spill and sat down. She could tell Frank was really fishing for a fight this morning and would have fished deeper had he not been so preoccupied with finding the lost pan. So rather than fishing, he just continued on his quest, moving from one side of the kitchen to another as if he was accomplishing great things. Banging steel against steel, wood against wood.

The noise, however abrasive and awful it was to Silvia, did serve the purpose of blocking her thoughts of yesterday, when she was fired from her job waiting tables in a Turkish cafe in downtown Philadelphia. She had overheard her boss say to the cook, "I'm going to have to close the place down if she works here another day!" And at hearing this, she marched into the kitchen and said, "I heard what you said Usef." She spoke to him as though he was wrong for being concerned for the survival of his business. Although he was, like most people, much bigger than her, he hunched over and shrunk like a frightened monkey at her confrontation. "I'm sorry Silvia," he said in his broken English, while looking down at the floor. And he really was sorry. Somewhere in the back of her head, she knew he was right. She was a coffee-spilling, plate-dropping wreck of a waitress who surprised herself the few times she got an order right.

"Why were you still working there anyway after you moved in with Dad?" said her older brother, Cosmo, in an effort to console her when she called him up right after she had been fired. As usual, he was right. It had made some

4

sense to continue her career as a bad waitress when she still lived in the city and the cafe was one block away from her place. But after she moved to Frank's house, it made no sense at all. She remained at the cafe, however, because jobs were hard to come by. When she told this to Cosmo, he said that she would find another "dead-end" job before she knew it. His attempt at consolation, while sincere, made her feel worse. Much worse. She needed no reminder of the fact that she had worked exclusively at dead end jobs since graduating from college two years ago.

She crumbled into a hunched over position and sipped her coffee that tasted markedly bitter. Just as she was slipping into a comfortable state of misery, Frank said, "Don't you have to be at work? It's eleven o'clock. What happened? Did you get canned again?" She was about to speak, when he swiftly picked up a broom and began chasing a centipede that was speeding across the floor.

"Those God damn bugs run around here like they own the place!" he shouted as it disappeared under a cabinet. He then threw the broom back in its corner as if he was angry at it. He picked up his half full drink, looked down as if he was studying it, and in a quick second, he finished it off. His insensitive remark seemed to have been wiped clean from his mind. She would have normally laughed his comment off, knowing well that it was only his way of attempting to instigate a fight. But a number of factors, including fatigue and getting fired from her job yesterday, conspired together to cause her to react.

"Why don't you have another drink?" she said facetiously.

He came alive like Frankenstein's monster, eyes bulging, face reddening and screamed back, "Why don't you get your stuff and get the fuck out of my house?!"

Her sarcastic response, "Because I know how much you'd miss me," heightened her father's anger, and his eyes bulged out so far they looked as if they might pop out of his head. He looked as if he was about to start screaming in the scariest of all his angry voices. His screams could make the house's walls vibrate. His voice was deep, guttural, heavy and carried long and far. So far, in fact, that she could still hear it no matter how far away she moved: Philadelphia, Brooklyn, Chicago, Tucson. Even when she took a summer backpacking trip through Europe, she could still hear his voice. She could tell by the look on his face that he was about to scream one of those vibrating-wall screams when his cell phone rang. He forcibly decompressed all that he could and walked quickly towards his phone, all the while still staring at Silvia, as if to say that that their little spat wasn't over yet. He answered the phone before the first ring ended and asked the caller if he had any information about the missing frying pan.

"How the hell should I know?" the voice on the phone said. "I don't even live with you!" The person on the other end spoke almost as loud as Frank, and Silvia could hear every word very clearly, as if he was standing right there in the kitchen.

Frank didn't bother apologizing for asking such an inappropriate question, nor did he ask his friend how he was doing. Rather, he just went right into his problems. He went through his usual list of complaints about his children: Vince spoke two words a year to him; Cosmo was a failure; and Angie broke his heart by moving to North Jersey. Silvia could tell that he was about to start in on her. But he glanced over and probably decided not to talk about her while she was sitting right there. So instead, he spoke about how all of his children's shortcomings were the fault of Donna, his wife, for being from a family with "bad genes."

When the voice on the phone asked about Donna, Frank walked into the other room so he could speak about his wife in private in his not-so-quiet, quiet voice. She had left him a little over one month ago. She had surprised herself and everyone around her by lasting as long as she did. Silvia suspected her mother would have left sooner, but had waited until her youngest child, Vince, was either out of the house or at least almost out of the house. She could hear Frank lying to the voice on the phone like he lied to everyone. She could hear him telling the voice that he and Donna just needed a little separation from each other, as if they had made some sort of mutual decision about how to proceed in their marriage. He walked back into the kitchen to freshen his drink and complained about the property taxes that would be due very soon. He ended his monologue of complaints with an expression he used frequently, "I can't complain."

Silvia thought that if Frank spent less time complaining and searching for lost kitchen utensils, he might notice the dilapidated condition of his house. The kitchen sink always leaked. The bathroom door handle fell off every time someone tried to open or close it. The floor creaked. The doors squeaked and hung on loose hinges from being slammed one too many times. The cracked paint struggled to cover the walls. The broken chandelier could fall at any second. While the house was falling apart, Frank's yard, in which he took great pride, was perfect. Not a bush out of place. Not one uneven blade of grass. All of the flowers and plants were lined up straight and were distanced apart from each other as if someone used a ruler to get them that way. His nice-looking red brick ranch style house sat on a pleasant tree lined street with other nice-looking houses with well-kept yards, though none were as well-kept as his own.

The house was on a street not far from the center of town and the town wasn't too far from Philadelphia, but not quite close enough to be considered a suburb. Frank would not set foot in the city even if it were five minutes away. To him, cities were nothing more than an added expense with their parking lots that cost ten dollars an hour and their expensive restaurants and shops full of useless, overpriced merchandise. He preferred the smallness of his own town with its practical shops and ample free parking. It was a real town too, the way towns used to be, with everything a person needed. It had a street that could have been named Main Street, with the same dress shop that had been there for over forty years; the same hardware shop for fifty years; the same grocery store for over sixty years; and the same bank that had been there for almost one hundred years.

Silvia loved the town in her own way. It was where she learned to ride a bike, where she had her first kiss from a boy, and where she spent long summer days with her grandma eating snow cones and playing hide-and-seek. She loved the town because it had an old-fashioned quality, as if it had been slightly stuck in time. But the town began to feel too small and intimate after she had moved away for college. After she had lived and traveled in so many exciting, international cities, it felt boring and provincial. By then, the town was nothing more than a place where she didn't belong, and she grew to resent it for making her into a misfit, a displaced person, and a girl without a hometown.

It was around this same time that her home stopped being her home and started being her father's house.

❧

She went into her bedroom, sat upon her bed, and stared into the blank space of hopelessness. She thought she would be protected from the racket in the kitchen, but the noise traveled fast and furiously down the long hallway to the twin-bedded room as if fueled by Frank's anxiety. The room offered no sanctuary, and she felt nothing for it despite that fact it was the first room that she had known and where she grew up. Perhaps because it was nothing more than a room inside of her father's house.

At one time, she and Angie had shared the room. Now all traces of Angie were gone, but evidence of Silvia remained in every corner of the room. Her childhood relics, like old picture books and My Little Ponies, were piled messily on her shelves. The radical junior prom dress, which she had made herself out of vintage floral curtains bought at an antique store, was still in her closet. Old concert tickets were tucked into her mirror frame, along with pictures of her with high school friends whose names she had forgotten. A collection of vinyl albums she inherited from her mother lived in one of the room's dusty corners, and some belongings from her present life, including art supplies and clothing, were shoved into another dusty corner. Her clothes were thrown in orange crates she obtained from a supermarket while at college. She refused to move her clothing into her old dresser so as to remind herself that the stay was very temporary. Besides, she had kept her clothes in these plastic containers for so long that they had grown familiar to her, and she had grown to like their familiarity. They fit in well with the rest of her disposable lifestyle of used futons, cheap clothing, and plastic kitchenware.

What if she took her clothes out of the orange crates and put them in the bureaus? Doing so would mean surrendering to the fact that she might be living with Frank indefinitely. Such a scenario was too painful to imagine. How could she have allowed herself to move back to this place for any period of time? She thought of what she should have done differently to avoid ending up here. She went through all of her mistakes in reverse chronological order that led to this point. First, she should have never been fired from her job. She wished that she had quit before she got fired. Better yet, she should have never taken the job in the first place. It had nothing more to offer her than free hummus and proximity to where she used to live. She would not have taken the job, or even applied for it, had she not lived so nearby. She would not have lived so nearby, if she had not moved in with her ex-boyfriend which was a huge mistake. She should have not had him as a boyfriend, but there was scanty choice of men in Philadelphia. This lack of selection brought her to her next regret, which was moving to Philadelphia. It was the third time that she had moved to this city. She didn't like it the first time she had lived there, and she liked it less and less with each move back.

She took a break from regretting to send an email to her friend Emily, who had just moved to Portland, Oregon, and who was encouraging Silvia to come join her. Silvia didn't need a lot of coaxing to move anywhere, let alone Portland, a place she already had her eye on. This would definitely be her next place. She had not even visited the city, but she was somehow sure that it was the place for her. Imagining herself in her new place gave her a much needed break from the dark, whirlwind of regrets that swirled around her. Yet, she was unable to stay in this fantasy world too long before the regret of leaving Tucson, the place she had lived before moving back to Philadelphia, hit her over the head. Moving from Tucson straight to Portland would have been so much easier than moving to Portland from New Jersey. She dreaded the long cross country trip she would probably be doing alone. She was ready to regret back even further to Chicago, Brooklyn, and eventually art school, when Vince appeared in the doorway of her room to ask if she wanted to get a slice of pizza.

"Pizza, huh?" she said, looking at her clock. "It's a little early for pizza, but I guess I can go for a slice." It dawned on her that he should be at school, but she didn't have the energy or concern to ask why he wasn't there. She barely had the energy to get up from her bed, but she thought that food might put some life back into her weakened body and knew there was no chance of getting a morsel of anything from Frank's kitchen, as long as he was anywhere in the house.

The two of them sneaked out of the house. If Frank noticed them leaving, he would ask them where they were going. They couldn't tell him that they were going to get something to eat, as he didn't tolerate anyone spending money on food outside of the house when there was perfectly good food at home. Even worse than leaving the house for food, was leaving Frank in the house alone. They both knew that he hated being left alone in the house. His reasoning was that he was an extrovert and enjoyed having people around him at all times. In fact, he strongly preferred the company of people with whom he was fighting than to being alone.

❧

As they exited the front door escaping Frank, the two of them synchronously sighed with relief. They walked into the lazy late spring air, where the trees drooped with heaviness and the smell of hyacinths lingered. Silvia's shabby clothes may have fit her mood perfectly, but they didn't match the sun shiny day. Despite her depressed mood and shabby clothes, she still brightened the space surrounding her. She moved through the world like a Peanut's character dancing. Vince moved in a straight line with precision, his head coming forward every few steps, making his shoulder length light brown hair come loose from behind his ears. He wasn't tall and wasn't short but was somewhere in between, and his eyes shone with purpose and determination. His left eyebrow curved upward like a Vulcan, making him look as if he was hiding something. But he hid nothing. He was an open book in large print.

They walked to Nina's Pizzeria only a few blocks from their house in a small strip mall. It didn't look like much from the outside or from the orange plastic inside, but it had the best pizza in town. Silvia ordered a piece of mushroom pizza and Vince got a slice of plain Sicilian. They were both vegetarian. Silvia had even been vegan for a while before discovering the horror of soy cheese.

"Hey Vince," said Silvia, while blotting the excess oil from her pizza with a napkin. "Why aren't you at school today?"

"Because I haven't missed one day of school all year, so I figured I was entitled to it. Besides, there's not much going on these last few days."

Silvia knew that he was telling the truth about only missing one school day all year. He was extremely conscientious and he never got sick. And, unlike the other Grecos, he never lied.

"You must be excited about going away to college," Silvia said, switching the subject.

"Kind of," Vince said as he chewed his pizza. He ate fast and nervous, as if somebody might take his food away at any second.

"So you're set on Berkeley?"

"They have the best sociology program in the country, so yeah, I'm set on going there. But not so excited about going so far away."

"I thought you'd want to get away from here," Silvia said, with a complete lack of understanding for why Vince or anyone would not want to go far away from Frank's house.

"Well, I've never been so far away, and Dad's not crazy about the idea of me going to school on the other side of the country. He keeps saying that he'll help, then he gets mad at me over nothing, and says that he won't help. I applied for all the loans I could and I told him I'd get residency right away so the tuition would be cheaper after the first year."

"Lucky that he even offered to help you at all. He barely helped me. If I didn't get a scholarship to college, I couldn't have gone. Guess I can't blame him, though, for not giving much help. He thought that an art degree would be completely useless. I'm starting to think he may have had something."

"You studied something you love," said Vince, eyes staring right into his sister's eyes. "There's nothing worthless about that." Silvia was often amazed at how her little brother was so advanced for his age. It seemed unusual, to the point of being weird, that a high school boy would care about making his older sister feel better about herself. He was such a good person, and his goodness came through loud and clear in all of his actions, like the way he refused to shop at Wal-Mart because of their "bad" politics, even though it was the only store of its kind in town; the way that he thanked their mother for cooking dinner every night; the way that he remained great friends with his ex-girlfriends, even if they were not so great to him.

It was sometimes hard for her to believe there was a time they didn't get along. However, had they always gotten along without a period of conflict, they would have been complete misfits in the Greco family. Silvia resented Vince as soon as he was born, for he replaced her position as the youngest child. He stole away all the attention she was used to getting for over four years, and even worse, he didn't acknowledge his theft. And he was by far the easiest and most pleasant of all the children. He wasn't hyper like Silvia was as a child, nor whiny like Angie, nor rebellious like Cosmo. He was the perfect child, the best saved for last, and Donna reminded her other children of this in her own quiet way.

Silvia stopped being resentful of Vince when she was about twelve and he was seven. He won her over by sharing half of his Halloween candy with her that year when she couldn't go trick or treating due to being sick with the flu. Only a seven-year-old child as exceptional as Vince would do such a thing. And Silvia felt that she had no choice at that point but to recognize that she was lucky to have him for a little brother, and any feelings of resentment or jealousy that were inside of her melted away.

They lived compatibly for a short while before they started becoming so much like each other that they grew competitive. They didn't compete about the usual stuff that siblings were inclined to compete about, like school grades. Instead, they competed with each other about who was more green or environmentally conscientious. They competed ferociously. Silvia made absolutely sure to recycle every single receipt she ever got, but Vince could clean up a spill in the kitchen with only half of a paper towel. Silvia took five-minute showers, but Vince would practically never set foot inside a car or vehicle of any sort. Silvia carried her own cloth bag with her so that she would never have to use a plastic bag, but Vince would not even purchase a product that was wrapped in plastic. So it was always a close draw. Now with Vince going to Berkeley, Silvia threw in the towel. She assumed that he was studying sociology because it would be a good major for his ambition of saving the world, but she thought she would ask him about it anyway.

"Why do you want to study sociology anyway?" Before he had a chance to answer the question, she added her own thoughts about choosing such a major. "It's one of those useless things to study, like painting. Not that I don't realize the value in studying what you have passion for and all. But living in poverty sucks. That's all I can tell you."

"I'm sure there's something you can do with your degree. What kind of job do you think you might like?" He cleverly redirected the course of the conversation so that he would not have to bother responding to her question, which Silvia knew would be a useless conversation. Trying to convince him of the uselessness of studying sociology was futile. In fact, trying to sway her brother of anything was virtually impossible. He was an extremely decisive and focused type of person. He was born knowing what he wanted out of life and knowing exactly how to get it. Silvia recalled the time that he was only five years old and the family went out for ice cream, and Vince knew that he wanted a blackberry flavored ice cream cone. How did he even know what blackberry was at the age of five, let alone know that he wanted ice cream of that particular flavor?

And now because of his short life-time of focus, determination, and absolute clarity, he had no need to talk about his own goals in life. So instead, he turned his attention to trying to work out his older sister's life. He had not even stepped foot in the world yet and didn't understand the whole career thing, as far as Silvia was concerned, and so his attempt at helping her with her life made her feel uncomfortable. But her feelings of awkwardness at discussing this subject didn't stop her from rambling on about all of the possible paths that she had, at one time or another, contemplated. She began with graphic design, a field she quickly dismissed as she would probably end up having to work in the advertisement industry. She thought of being a college professor, but that was way too much of a long and arduous pursuit. She very briefly thought of becoming a museum curator or archivist, but thought that that she would never find a job as one. And lastly, she mentioned a billboard painter, which she added only as a joke.

"I like the college professor idea myself. You'd be following in Mom's footsteps. She'd like that."

"Yeah, but like I said, it's a long path. And after that big investment of time and money and energy, I'd probably be lucky to find a job in Kansas."

"Well yeah, but finding a job shouldn't be the most important thing." Now his youth and inexperience and naiveté were showing through. Finding a job is not important when you have no concept of things like rent and health insurance. He was young and idealistic, and probably had no concrete ideas of what he planned on doing with a sociology degree. In fact, when Silvia asked him about his choice of study, he said that he wasn't sure exactly what he would do with such a degree, but he knew that it would give him the best foundation for doing something where he could really make a difference in the world at large.

"I can't just stand by and watch the world continue to deteriorate the way it is," he added like the superhero he was. His eyes filled with so much sincerity that it was almost painful to look at him.

Silvia wasn't sure of his exact plan for saving the world, and from what she could tell, either was he. Part of her wanted to warn him more about trying to save an irredeemable world and about studying something so impractical and useless. But the bigger part of her knew he needed to fall on his own face. She only hoped that he would not have to fall as hard as she had. In the meantime, why shouldn't he enjoy the good times? The dreaming, the cheering, the trying. So instead of giving him any lectures on the topic of self-preservation, she commended him for his lofty ambitions.

"Well that's great Vince," she said, making her face as serious and hopeful as possible.

Vince smiled modestly, and then looked down at Silvia's slice of pizza, which was only half eaten. She had sprinkled hot pepper flakes on it, hoping that this addition would make it more appetizing, but it still tasted like everything else had been tasting to her since she had been in this slump– like nothing.

"Not hungry?" he said.

"I have no appetite lately," she said. "Do you want the rest?"

Vince gladly took the rest of the pizza. While he ate, he looked around their table conspiratorially and spotted a couple eating, what appeared to be a pepperoni pizza. Silvia knew, from the mild condescension in his eyes, that her brother was thinking about how awful it was that they were eating meat. And like her, he might also imagine the awful existence led by the pig that made the pepperoni possible. She sometimes felt as if their two separate minds became one.

"Oh shit," Silvia said, sliding down into her seat to make herself less visible, "I went out with that guy in high school." She was referring to the young man who just walked into the pizza place. His name was Al Santora, and she was dismayed to see that he looked really good.

"Don't turn around," she said to Vince, who unfortunately had already turned around, and in doing so, had caught the attention of Al, who, in turn, stared back at the table at which they sat. It was too late to pretend that she didn't see him. Their eyes had already exchanged glances, and now he was walking towards their table. He was dressed in a grey suit and tie with a checkered button down shirt, and had extremely bright eyes that went perfectly with his teeth that looked as if they had been painted with Wite-Out. He was very different from Silvia, like all of her ex-boyfriends, and this could have been why she was attracted to him.

"Silvia!" he said as he walked towards the table. She forced a smile that she knew looked strained and unnatural.

"Hey Al. Good to see you," she lied.

"Yeah, you too," he said. "How are things?"

"Things are great," she lied again, and then quickly asked how he was doing before he had a chance to ask her any more questions about her own life.

"Couldn't be better," he said, exhaling as if his body couldn't contain all of the happiness and well-being inside of it.

"Oh, you remember my little brother, Vince?" she said, gesturing to Vince before Al had a chance to tell her about how great his life was.

"I do remember," said Al, "not so little anymore."

Silvia and Vince laughed out of courtesy. Al then looked at his watch in the way that all busy, successful people look at their watches, and said that he had to be off to a meeting. Silvia was more than happy to see him go and thrilled that she didn't have to hear about his current life situation. She imagined that it was much better than being unemployed and living with a crazy parent.

She then tried to remember why she broke up with Al. He was a nice enough guy. Most girls would not have found a thing wrong with him. But Silvia wasn't like most girls. She found whatever she could find wrong with a guy and would leave him for the next one who came along.

"He has bad taste in music," she once whined to Cosmo about a boyfriend with whom she wanted to break up.

"How bad?" asked Cosmo.

"He likes jam bands!"

"Oh, that is bad," agreed Cosmo with complete seriousness, "you should break up with him."

છ૭

When Silvia and Vince returned to the house, Frank was sleeping in the den in front of a blaring television set, snoring loud and rhythmic. Even when he slept, he was loud. He snored and squirmed and tossed and rattled. He slept in the den probably more than he slept in his own bed, especially since Donna had left. The room was dark and cozy, and had a long red plaid couch that stretched from one side of the room to the other. The built-in shelves were filled with his books from college and law school, with a smattering of Plato and Dickens and legal codes. These reminded Frank of his accomplishments and of who he was.

"He's passed out for the count," said Vince, as he always said when Frank was passed out.

"I think he has court tonight," said Silvia, semi-worried. Frank worked as a judge in a local courthouse, and despite the fact that his family life was a wreck, his professional life was quite together. He shined as a judge just as he had shined as a lawyer. Silvia had gone to court with him on occasion and was almost unable to recognize the distinguished man who sat before the courtroom.

"Don't worry. He'll be up in time. He always is. He's never late."

"Oh yeah," said Silvia, as she recalled that Frank never needed an alarm clock. This wasn't true of herself. Waking up was always difficult for Silvia, even with an alarm clock. She was inclined to push the snooze button several times after the buzz went off. She had tried moving the clock across the room from her so that she would be forced to get up out of bed to turn it off. But this never quite worked out. She would get up and go over to the clock to push the snooze button and then drag the clock closer to her bed so that she could proceed to push the snooze several more times. It was no wonder that she was perpetually late for everything.

She and Vince went into their respective rooms and closed the doors, which was another thing that Frank hated and didn't understand. "Why are people always closing doors in this God Damn house?" he would say. He liked open doors. He thought that there was nothing to hide. He figured that his children closed doors because they had inherited a bad gene from Donna's side of the family that caused them to be introverted. Silvia thought that Frank often confused things, and that in this case, he confused independence with introversion. She thought that her mother and siblings enjoyed being alone for the same reason that cats like being alone– because they were independent. She also thought that Frank was sorely mistaken in thinking that any of her mother's family members were introverted, and Donna, herself, least of all. On occasion, she could even be gregarious.

Frank possibly mistook his wife's seriousness for introversion. She was a serious person, too serious to be bothered with incidental things like small talk or the conventions of conversation. And tonight, when she called Silvia, she wasted no time getting right to the point.

"Hi Silvie, dear," she said in a low voice. "I'm worried about Vince." Silvia could see her mother sitting in her very tiny studio apartment that overlooked Rittenhouse Square. It was in a high rise with a neat, clean and simple, blandly colored beige and off white interior. She moved into the place, after leaving Frank, at the suggestion of a colleague who lived in the very same building. When Silvia had last seen it, she was struck by its complete lack of decorations. It looked more like a hotel room than a place where a person lived. Silvia wondered if her mother had not made any attempts to decorate because she was intent on getting back with Frank, or because the rent was too expensive for her to afford long term and that she had planned on leaving it for a cheaper apartment. Silvia assumed that the apartment was more than her mother could afford on her part-time college professor salary.

Aside the financial stress that Silvia imagined her mother must have felt, she was also surely stressed over leaving before Vince had graduated high school and was safely out of the house. Every time she and Silvia had spoken since she left Frank, Vince had been the focal point of their conversation.

"He sounds depressed when I talk to him on the phone. And last weekend, when I saw him, he moped around the whole time. I know he's not mad at me. I didn't do anything to make him mad, and he doesn't get mad. You know the way he is. He could be depressed. I really hope Dad isn't being a total bastard to him."

Silvia was hurt by her mother's lack of concern for how she was doing. Yet, she was relieved that she didn't have to delve into her problems, because each time she did, they seemed to grow like a big pile of trash getting higher because of a garbage strike. Feeling hurt, while understandable, was rare for Silvia. She never seemed to need anything from anyone, including her own mother, and never felt hurt for someone's lack of concern for how she was doing. But she was at an all-time low and so she felt hurt. Of course, she made no display of her hurt feelings but rather listened to her mother continue with her monologue of worry. She told her mother that Vince was just nervous about going so far away to college and about the possibility of Frank not paying.

"Dad will pay. He just likes to threaten that he won't. And as far as going so far away is concerned, you think he'd be happy to get as far away from that house as possible!" Donna said. Although Silvia couldn't agree with her mother more about how Vince should be happy to get far away, this comment caused her to sink even further down. Fortunately, her mother caught her insensitivity.

"I'm sorry, Silvie. I didn't mean to put the house down. Besides, you're only staying there until you get yourself together. You could stay with me here."

"In your little studio Mom? Where would I sleep? In the bathtub?"

"Well, you're much better at dealing with Dad than I was. And you're much better than Vince."

"He and Dad are getting along fine Mom," she said.

"I don't believe that, Silvie."

"Well then I'm not sure what to tell you."

"Hey, didn't that weird girl he was seeing break up with him a little while ago?"

"I don't know. He doesn't talk about that stuff to me. I don't know if he discusses his love life with anyone. I just think he's anxious about going far away."

Then Donna blurted out, "I bet that Dad is trying to turn Vince against me. Turn a son against his own mother. Imagine that. Do you hear Dad mentioning my name at all to Vince?"

Silvia could very clearly picture the indignant expression on her mother's still youthful face.

"No, I didn't hear him mention your name to Vince, Mom."

"It's just that I always worry about Vince. Oh, I wish I could have stayed there longer, but I just couldn't."

"You don't have to explain yourself to me, Mom," said Silvia with a hint of sarcasm.

"Maybe he thinks I was neglectful."

"He doesn't think that, Mom."

"Maybe I can plan some kind of party for his graduation. That would be a way to make it up to him."

"Make what up to him?" Despite Silvia's frustration, she was beginning to accept the fact that her mother wasn't listening to her, so she decided to stop talking and to let Donna rant on freely.

"Yes, it can be something simple. We can plan for a family dinner at a nice restaurant." She cleverly inserted the word *we* where the word *I* should have been to draft Silvia into helping her with the party she was planning.

Of course, Silvia would help her mother. It was difficult to refuse her. For starters, she felt sorry for her for being married to Frank. And now, after being with the same person for just about all of her adult life, she would have to start over. The thought of her mother being trapped between the guilt of leaving Vince and the pain of living with Frank made Silvia want to do whatever she could do to help. Although she couldn't refuse her, she did wish that Donna had asked someone else for help. But who would she ask? Cosmo was in his own world, and Angie kept her distance from their mother. So it was up to Silvia.

Besides, she knew that she was the only one in her family that would be able to accomplish this great feat. All the Greco family members had not been together for over six years, since Angie's wedding. Cosmo couldn't hide his life-long resentment of Angie. Donna couldn't hide her sadness for being so distant from her bride daughter. Frank couldn't hide his sadness for losing the only child he was close to, and this was expressed in the tear-filled drunk toast he gave before the dinner. She thought of all the past holidays that they had spent together. She could only remember two Christmases that Frank didn't rage, which was compensated with siblings fighting each other. She could only recall one family gathering that didn't involve fighting. During the extremely rare gatherings that didn't involve a fight, the threat of one hung in the air like the sword of Damocles. For Silvia, this threat was worse than a fight. It made a knot in her stomach that took over her entire body.

She imagined what a graduation party for Vince might look like. Frank would be drunk and determined to make trouble. He would show his blatant favoritism towards Angie in hopes of making his other children resent her. He would make Donna extremely tense and uncomfortable. He would remind Cosmo of what a failure he was for dropping out of University of Pennsylvania. And he would remind Vince of how he had better be on his best behavior if he wanted help with his tuition. Angie would brag about how her family lived in a three million dollar home in the same neighborhood as Bruce Springsteen. Vince didn't like her husband Doug because he worked as an investor for Goldman Sachs. Cosmo and Angie's bad feelings towards each other, which stemmed back to their childhoods, could have an opportunity to be further nurtured. Donna and Angie could feel their distance from each other, and Silvia would dream about leaving this mess of a family once and for all.

Yet, Silvia noticed a shining light in the darkness of imagining. Since she began thinking about the gathering, she had not been thinking about her own problems. She felt good for the first time in a long time. She was now a person with a purpose, and an altruistic purpose at that. She was looking out for her mother and her little brother. And in getting everyone together, she was attempting to make peace in a family that had never known peace.

She then noticed the way her body lightened and her stomach opened and was crying out for food. She craved a big bowl of pastina with butter and salt. Pastina was what she ate whenever she was getting over a stomach flu. Pastina was what she ate when she couldn't eat anything else. Pastina was one of the things that Grandma Tucci used to make for her when she was a child. Entering the kitchen, Silvia felt ecstatic to find a half full box of De Cecco stellette pasta sitting in one of the cupboards and was even more ecstatic that Frank was out of the house. Although she continued to be apprehensive about him barging in at any second while she ate her pastina, she was able to taste her food and enjoy the act of eating for the first time in a long time.

CHAPTER 2

WHAT'S WRONG WITH HERE?

Factory smoke puffed into the gray sky that hung over Philadelphia as Silvia drove over the Ben Franklin Bridge. The sun had been trying to peak through all morning and it finally gave up. But today, Silvia didn't need the sun. She felt bright and shiny enough inside herself since her phone conversation with Donna last night. She now had a whole new sense of purpose and didn't care that she was on her way to one of her art school modeling jobs, which usually depressed her. Such jobs were fine when she was a student, but now that she had graduated and had a degree, it was beneath her. In addition to it requiring no skill, it wasn't very dignified or interesting to be standing naked in front of a bunch of art students, who she now perceived as overly privileged and sheltered despite the fact that she was one of them not so long ago. It was, however, the only job she had until something else came up. She was afraid that that 'something else' would probably end up being a job near her father's house.

She drove to south Philly to park her car. This section of the city was easily over two miles from the art college, but it had street parking spots that, while not ample, were free. The college itself was in the downtown section of the city that only had paid lots that Silvia couldn't afford. She tapped the bumpers of the cars in front and in back of her as she crammed into a space that was way too small for her car. Her hatchback had faded to the palest shade of yellow from the Tucson sun, was covered with dents and scratches, and had one mismatched panel colored off-white on the front left hand side. She wasn't concerned with the looks of her car and thought its shabby appearance as a good thing for deterring potential thieves. Internally, the car was fit, and that was what mattered most. She did whatever maintenance she could do on her own, for Frank had instilled within her a mistrust of auto-mechanics and warned her, that as a young woman, she was extremely susceptible to their tricks.

After parking her car, she began on her long walk to the college. In south Philly, she passed row homes, corner bodegas, and people who looked like they might have lived on the same street for their entire lives. As she got closer to the downtown, the space surrounding her gradually filling with skyscrapers, Starbucks, sidewalk preachers, people sleeping on the street, and fast walking professionals. As she got into the downtown, the smell of cheese steaks, that permeated the air in south Philly, changed into a less distinct flavor of urban stench.

When she was only a couple of blocks from the college, she heard someone scream her name and she was happily surprised to see it was Rafa, a guy she met at an anti-war protest a few years back. He was a thin fellow with brown skin, black almond eyes, and a head of afro-hair that made him look like he belonged in the seventies.

"Hey Rafa," she said. "It's great to see you."

"You too. What are you doing downtown?" he said while inconspicuously inspecting her from head to toe.

"Oh, just meeting a friend for lunch," she said, still reluctant to talk about her current life situation to anyone. She was quick to ask him about himself in hopes of diverting any attention away from herself.

"I'm bartending at Dirty Frank's up the street. And I've been going to the Occupy rallies when I can. And, oh, you'll love this. I took a couple of woodworking classes and I've been building all kinds of stuff. Chairs and tables and boxes."

"Wow that's great," said Silvia feeling slightly envious of him for his apparent happiness. She tried to think of some kind of follow up question to ask him about his newfound craft, but her mind was blank.

"How's your little brother doing?" said Rafa squinting into the sun. "I remember you brought him to a couple of the protests."

This question spurred a mini conversation about Vince and college and Berkeley, and ended with Rafa giving Silvia his phone number and telling her to give him a call some time if she wanted to go for coffee. She said that she would, though she knew that she probably wouldn't be calling him. He was certainly cute and nice enough. There was just something about him that seemed boring. In addition to that excuse, she was sure that she would be moving to Portland soon and didn't want to get involved with anyone in this area.

She wasn't expecting to run into anyone else from her past, but as she was about to enter the college, she unluckily ran into a former classmate, Kayla, who studied graphic design, the practical art school major. Silvia had trouble relating to the graphic design majors, as they were too modern for her. She preferred vinyl records to CDs, print books to e-books, and paintbrushes and canvas to a computer. Kayla was long and narrow and had her hair tied in a knot that sat perfectly on the top of her pointy-head. She was always stylish and elegant, even dressed down in jeans and sneakers like she was today. Silvia tried to dodge her by pretending that she didn't see her, but her efforts were in vain.

"Hi Silvia," Kayla said, smiling with eyes open wide. "What you are doing here?"

"Just visiting," Silvia said, wondering when she would be able to stop lying to people about herself. "And you?"

"Just had to pick up some transcripts," she said with a smile that showcased her super straight and sparkling teeth. "I'm starting grad school in the fall." Her rich parents would undoubtedly be paying, Silvia thought.

"That's great," said Silvia smiling fraudulently.

Kayla then proceeded to update her on the current status of various other students in their class who were all doing "really well." Some were earning good salaries; others pursuing their life-long dreams. Others were working in jobs that, while not well paying, were internally rewarding. Silvia's state of hopelessness, that had lessened only just last night, was now rising fast and steep. She was relieved when Kayla said that she had to go.

ↄↄ

The classroom where Silvia was modeling was big and white and full of students, most dressed in faded jeans and paint covered clothing. In the room were dusty tables, clay for sculpting, and a variety of other supplies scattered messily and piled high on any available shelves. She would be modeling for a very long and boring anatomy class with all of the students examining her little body like it was some sort of lab specimen. She greeted the professor and quickly went down the hall to a bathroom to undress and put on a terry cloth bathrobe to wear in the classroom during her few short breaks.

Standing naked in front of a bunch of strangers didn't bother Silvia in the slightest. But she was bothered by the strain of holding one position for an extended period of time, sometimes as much as twenty minutes. Anatomy was a required course for sophomores. As it didn't interest her, she had ample opportunity to contemplate her problems, to hear Kayla's annoyingly cheerful voice saying that their class mates were doing "really well" along with her father's beaten down grumbling voice saying, "It's no wonder you can't do anything with your life." Maybe he was right. She stared back at the art students resentfully for having no missed opportunities and no regrets at this point in their young lives.

She was descending into that dark hole once again, and with time moving excruciatingly slow, she found it difficult to not look at the clock every two minutes. To make the minutes pass faster, she thought about her move to Portland. She had decided that Portland was definitely the perfect place for her, and she had come to this decision by using process of elimination. She broke the country into major sections, eliminated them one by one, and was left with the northwest. She could hear Cosmo telling her that it was absurd to evaluate an entire region as one place instead of breaking it down city-by-city or even state-by-state.

"You can't dismiss a whole region just like that!" he would say.

But once again, she ignored her brother's advice. She began with the northeast section of the country, which she quickly dismissed as old and stale and boring and filled with too many memories and old associations for her to start clean. She dismissed the southeast as creepy and too slow and filled with weird bugs. She dismissed the southwest for the same reason that she dismissed the mid-west, that being the fact that she had already lived there. Besides, one was too hot and one was too cold. California just seemed stupid and expensive and overpopulated. So that left the northwest, with Seattle and Portland the only two cities she would consider. Seattle was so nineties. She was normally not concerned with being fashionable. She dressed like a sixties chick and listened to British Invasion bands, but when it came to places, fashion was important. And Portland was now recognized as the greenest city in the country, so by moving there, she might get ahead of Vince in their green competition.

She was about to imagine how she would get there, when the instructor ordered her to change positions. She quickly changed positions and got right back to her planning. She would have to drive, but didn't want to drive alone. She had taken one too many road trips alone. As she contemplated the possibility of having to take another solo trip to get to Portland, her mind got flooded with a bunch of bad memories of previous solo trips: A scary stare from some rape artist-looking guy in Birmingham while at a gas station; camping through a vicious lightning storm outside of Toledo; some creepy big trucker who asked her if she had any plans for the night while checking into a motel near Dallas; the blow out she got as she approached El Paso; driving through a rain storm in Little Rock while giant sized droplets banged hard and angrily upon her little car; driving on dead E for miles and miles in the New Mexican desert before finding a gas station.

"Change positions," said the instructor again, forcing her to halt her rambling mind that went right back into rambling after she changed positions. She thought about staying in South Jersey until she had enough money to buy a plane ticket to Portland and to pay to have her car transported across the county on a truck. But who knew when that would be? It could be well over a year before she had that kind of money. The notion of living in South Jersey for such a long period of time frightened her more than all of her scary road memories put together. Much more.

She thought that she might ask Cosmo if he would come with her. Maybe even move out there with her. She didn't consider the sacrifice he would have to make in leaving his job and finding a new one. She was so used to moving to new places, having to get jobs right away, and finding one within a few days of her arrival. She thought about what job she might get in Portland. She could hear Cosmo saying something about finding a dead end job. Surely, he was right. It would be dead end. As she began to consider the job that she might have to take in Portland, her head began to hurt and her stomach felt nauseous. She looked up at the clock to find that she had not looked at it in over twenty minutes and felt a great sense of accomplishment. The class was almost over, so she could get out of this place soon and head over to Cosmo's.

∽

Cosmo's apartment was situated not far from the University he had attended over six years ago. He spent two years making good grades in tough courses without much studying. Then one day, he just dropped out. He gave no reason. Just said that he was bored of going to classes. He continued working and living near the college and had managed to make something of a life. According to Silvia, it wasn't much of one. She wasn't exactly sure what he did for a job, but he told her that monkeys could be trained to do it. He did, however, seem to like his monkey work in that it required very little of him.

The lobby of his apartment building was run down and dingy with lime green carpets and florescent lights. When Silvia arrived at his door on the second floor, Cosmo let her in, sat down, and continued playing some video game that she apparently had interrupted. She ignored his lack of social grace and went straight over to the window to open the curtains. The curtains were always drawn tight in his apartment, making the place dark even on the brightest of days. Cosmo didn't seem to notice or care about the darkness or the grunginess of his apartment. The furniture looked as if it came from various dumpster diving excursions. He hid spots or cracks on his walls by taping star maps in front of such imperfections. His shelves were crammed with beaten up science fiction and astronomy books; his floors were filled with everything from tattered comic books to video games consoles. In one of his corners stood a white and aqua marine colored electric guitar that he had taught himself to play, with great ease, while still in high school. His tables were covered with dirty coffee cups and little plastic, painted Tolkienesque figurines.

After opening the curtains, Silvia removed a smashed bug on the wall, which had been there the last time she visited him over a week ago.

"That's disgusting Cosmo," she said, removing the bug from the wall with a paper towel she got from the kitchen.

"What?" he said without looking up from his game. He probably had not even noticed the bug. He was, in fact, oblivious to most everything around him, and Silvia supposed it had something to do with his brilliance. "Cosmo's so smart that he forgets to comb his hair," Donna would say. His hair was a wild mess of not-yet-grayed Einstein hair going in all directions like palm trees fronds. He dressed himself in whatever he could find. Today it happened to be an old pair of jeans, an orange tee shirt, and a blazer style jacket that made no sense with the rest of his getup and was too short on his tall lanky body.

"Oh that bug," he said grinning. "I was waiting for you to come over. I thought we might give it a proper burial."

"Very funny," said Silvia.

"You hungry?" he went into the kitchen and opened his cabinets, revealing so many cans of tuna fish stacked high on top of each other that it looked as if he might be expecting a natural catastrophe to strike at any minute.

"I brought my own food," said Silvia, taking out an individual sized container of rice milk and a box of organic cookies with no dairy, no sugar, no wheat, and no soy. She offered one to Cosmo, who took one bite of one of the cookies and curled his face up in disgust.

"These taste like tree bark," he said, swallowing his one small bite as if it was killing him.

"Well, I like them, and that's all I care about," said Silvia, taking Cosmo's dislike of her cookies as a rejection. He went over to his refrigerator, walking in his usual manner with a bounce in his step and his head bopping back and forth like a song. By the looks of the ingredients he got out and put on the table, Silvia assumed that he was planning to make tuna fish and spaghetti, an old family favorite that Donna had learned from her mother.

"You should take it easy on the tuna fish, you know. It has a lot of mercury in it," said Silvia, sitting down at Cosmo's small white kitchen table.

"Yeah, I should," replied Cosmo, completely unconvinced by Silvia's warning. She was always warning about something: Cell phones, nitrates, trans-fats, slouching, the sun.

"You can get mercury poisoning. Doesn't that worry you?" said Silvia.

"Ah," said Cosmo. He paused to look at the ceiling as though he was really contemplating this question, and then came back with a definitive, "No!"

"Have you talked to Vince?" asked Silvia.

"No, how's he doing?" said Cosmo, as he filled a big soup pot with water.

"He's nervous about going so far away and he's nervous that Dad won't help with his tuition, and he can't get financial aid because Dad makes too much. So he's not doing so great."

"Oh, don't worry about Dad. He just likes to string people along. I bet he'll help him after all is said and done." He began chopping garlic and tomatoes on a cutting board.

Frank favored Cosmo least of all his children, and Silvia was always struck by how indifferent Cosmo often seemed to the lack of favoritism shown to him by their father. Frank formulated his opinion of Cosmo before he was even born, when Donna was pregnant with him and decided to name him after her father. Her father's name was Cosimo, and she had changed the spelling slightly, but it wasn't enough of a change for Frank. Frank and Donna's father disliked each other from their very first meeting. Silvia could only assume that this was because they were so similar. Like Frank,

Cosimo was always ready for a fight, and like Frank, he had a very strong presence. Silvia could always tell when her Grandpa Tucci was around, even if he didn't speak a word or make a sound. Perhaps Frank would have liked his first-born son if he had had a different name, and then perhaps Cosmo would like Frank back. Frank would have given his son all of the support and encouragement that he needed. Cosmo would have stayed in school because making his father proud would have been important to him. Frank would not have to spend years after his son dropped out of college speaking the same refrain, "He could have done something with his life!" And Cosmo would have probably been working as a researcher for NASA or doing some kind of comparable job. But Cosmo was given his cursed name, and with it, a lifetime of being resented by his own father. Silvia suspected that Frank may also have been jealous of Cosmo's brilliance. He couldn't, for the life of him, figure out from whom his son got that science gene, but he surely assumed it was inherited from someone on the Greco side.

"I can see Vince in Berkeley," said Cosmo, stirring spaghetti into a big pot of boiling water. "He'll fit right in with all his causes."

"He wants to save the world," Silvia added.

"The world's too late for saving," said Cosmo as he opened a can of tuna.

46

"That's exactly what I think," said Silvia, enthusiastic about her and her brother's like-mindedness. Cosmo, however, didn't seem at all surprised that they had the same thought. He wasn't moved or shaken by much, kind of like a big rock that sits on the shore and does not move, even when a gigantic wave sweeps over it.

"I guess he's got to be true to himself," said Cosmo, with skeptical eyes and a slight grin.

"Well, I was thinking we should have some kind of gathering for him, like a graduation party. Mom thinks it would be a good thing too. She suggested it."

"I'm surprised she's not nervous about seeing Dad. I sure as hell don't want to see him. Or Angie."

"Well, I'm sure she is, but her feelings for Vince might outweigh her apprehension about seeing Dad."

"If we have it at home, she'll be really uneasy. We might have to have it in a restaurant, and you know Dad isn't going to want to pay for anything out."

"Well maybe we can go some place cheap. I don't know, a pizzeria or something," said Silvia leaning forward in her chair.

"You think Angie will come down here for a pizzeria?" he said sarcastically while stirring the spaghetti.

"Well, all I'm saying is it would be nice to have a something for Vince where everybody is getting along, or at least pretending to get along. He's nervous about going so far away, and Dad keeps changing his mind about helping with his tuition, and Mom thinks he's really depressed and it would be nice to have something before he leaves for college." She said all this without taking a gasp for air.

"Yeah it would be nice, but I'm not sure how likely a nice, peaceful gathering of our family will be." He placed the tuna, garlic, and tomatoes into a heated frying pan filled with olive oil.

"Well we can try," she said frustratingly and left the room for the bathroom. When she returned, Cosmo was situated in front of the television set with a huge bowl of spaghetti and tuna fish.

"I'd offer you some, but I know you don't want any," he said through his smacking.

"You're right about that," she said walking over to the TV, on top of which was a DVD of Monty Python's *The Life of Brian*. She picked it up and looked back at her brother, who then recommended that they watch it. So they did. She felt relief at the idea of watching a movie and being able to forget about her problems for a little while. But at the end of the movie, when the song "Always Look on the Bright Side of Life" played, she slumped down into her seat and started to think of her own life and wonder why, with all that she had to be happy about, she was unable to look on the bright side of life. She was well aware of the potential harshness of reality and knew that her own life was, relatively speaking, a great life. She read the news that was filled with nothing but war and tragedy and catastrophes. She walked plenty of city streets where she had seen homeless people freezing to death before her eyes, wearing trashcan clothes on their broken bodies. She had no real problems, except for her cursed tendency to see what was wrong with things and, in particular, places. A tendency she had cultivated like a garden of rotten flowers. A tendency that caused her to want to leave wherever she was.

"Have you ever been to Portland?" she asked Cosmo, breaking the trend of thought in her head.

"Portland, Maine or Portland, Oregon?" he asked.

"Portland, Oregon, of course," she said, as if it should have been perfectly apparent to him which one she was talking about.

"Can't say that I have."

She waited a few seconds for him to ask her why she was asking him if he had ever been there, but when he didn't say anything, she said, "Well, I'm thinking about moving there."

"What else is new?" Cosmo said, sitting back in his seat.

"What's that supposed to mean?" said Silvia, with a fighting look on her face.

"You move all the time, Silvia."

"Well, so what if I do? It doesn't hurt anyone."

"So, why Portland? Have you ever been there?" Cosmo asked as if he knew what her answer would be.

"No, I haven't. But I have a friend who just moved there, and she loves it. And I've never heard anything but good about it. It's always rated highly in all those books about places to live. And it's supposed to have great public transportation. And..."

Cosmo cut her off probably because he knew, that if he didn't cut her off, he would be sitting there all night while she rationalized her next relocation.

"So, why do you want to move there?" he asked with emphasis on the word *you*.

"Because it's where everyone is moving to," she said, trying to convince herself of her answer.

"No, I mean what's in it for you?" asked Cosmo.

"What's in any place?" asked Silvia.

"Exactly," said Cosmo.

"I don't get it," said Silvia, who was beginning to get very frustrated with the way the conversation was going.

"What's wrong with here?" said Cosmo.

"By here, I assume you mean Philadelphia?" said Silvia, and then continued on with her answer to the question before giving Cosmo an opportunity to clarify what he meant. "I'm not even sure where to begin. For one thing, it's fucking filthy. It smells like piss and garbage everywhere. It's provincial. And has a high crime rate. And well, it's just gross."

She was preparing to continue with her rant, when Cosmo interrupted and said, "Maybe if you were doing something you liked to do, you wouldn't care so much about where you are."

Silvia was about to be vindictive and degrade Cosmo's entire existence by saying something to the effect of him being one to talk about doing something he liked. As far as she could see, he was wasting his life away by working a routine job that was beneath him intellectually, by spending his spare time playing video games, and by going out with women who he didn't really seem to like. But she stopped herself as she knew deep down inside that he was only trying to help. Besides, she had already done a pretty good job bashing the city in which he lived. Without being willing to put her brother down, she felt deprived of a rebuttal to his silly belief that if she was doing something she liked, this area would suddenly and magically transform into a great place. But then she thought of something to say in her defense.

"I love to paint and I do it almost every day. What about that?"

"I mean a job you like," said Cosmo.

"Well, maybe I will pursue that path someday, but I'm not doing it here," said Silvia, folding her arms and looking up at the ceiling.

"So, you have to be in Portland to do that?" said Cosmo with a jaded expression on his face, as if this wasn't, by any means, the first time that they had had this discussion.

"No, I don't have to be there necessarily. But I can't be here! I won't be here! I'm not staying in this fucking city or anywhere in the area for that matter!"

"You talk about it like it's Baghdad," said Cosmo.

"I know it's not that bad. It's just that I don't feel inspired here."

"Then why did you leave Tucson and come back here?" said Cosmo.

"Those summers there were killers," she said immediately, as if she had her response all prepared for some time now.

"What about New York?"

"It was too expensive. It's no place for an artist anymore. All the rich people drove the artists out. Same in any big, overrated, overpriced city," she said as if she had rehearsed this excuse several times as well.

"And Chicago?"

"Have you ever experienced a Chicago winter? They're absolutely brutal."

"And Philly is out for reasons you already stated?" said Cosmo, not expecting an answer, and then continued with, "What about the south? Atlanta? It's cheaper down there."

Silvia looked at him with cynical eyes, "Would you live in the south? A bunch of rednecks down there that say eye-talian."

"So, you'll get to Portland and decide that you don't like it there. It won't take you long to find something wrong with the place, and then you'll get depressed, and you'll come back here and get some shit job, and maybe move in with Dad again because you'll be broke."

There was a short silence after Cosmo's little prophecy that seemed very long and noisy to Silvia, who had suddenly developed the kind of lump in her throat that precedes tears, but because she wasn't a crier, she got angry with Cosmo and stormed out of his apartment without saying a word. Cosmo must have known that any attempts to dissuade her from leaving would be in vain. He was inclined to make blunt, insensitive remarks, like the time that he said the only kind of jobs Silvia could ever hang on to were those at book stores and health food stores. Silvia actually appreciated his sense of honesty and could usually tolerate his remarks as long as they were not about her one and only sensitive spot, which was her inability to stay in one place.

She knew that Cosmo, like everyone else in her life, could never understand how painful it was for her to be still. She thought of the times that she had wanted to stay put in a place for longer than a few months, but she simply couldn't. Whenever she planned on moving to a new place, she intended it to be her last move, but she knew somewhere in the back of her mind, that it would not be her last. The very thought of staying put in one place frightened her. While most people were stressed by the prospect of moving to a new place, she was stressed by having to stay in the same one. When she occasionally had to stay for longer than a few months out of financial strain, she felt like a lion she had once seen that had been ruthlessly placed in a very small cage in a rundown zoo somewhere in Arizona.

As she walked down the street to her car, taking fast and angry footsteps, stewing over Cosmo's remarks, she came across a neon sign that said *Psychic Reader* that she must have passed by several times before, but had not noticed until now. She always laughed at psychics, and the desperate people who patronized their businesses. But, right now she felt so lost and desperate that she was actually considering going into the psychic shop. She quickly knocked on the door, before she had a chance to reconsider paying the fortuneteller a visit, and then waited for almost an entire minute for some lady in a flowing scarf to come to the door, but there was nothing. So she knocked again, and this time her knocks were hard and loud. Still, there was no answer. So she peeked in to see some pudgy lady stuffed into a pair of very unfashionable stone washed jeans, sleeping in front of a television set with an opened phone book thrown over her face to block the light. This was, undoubtedly, the all-knowing psychic.

$\curlyvee\curlyveedownarrow$

The drive back to Jersey was short, but seemed long on this particular night. Silvia was especially upset by having to spend her last four dollars on the bridge toll and by missing her exit because of her preoccupation with her anger at Cosmo. She was beginning to think that Frank was right about her brother. He was a failure and would never amount to much of anything. Yet, she knew that her brother's prediction about her life was true– that she would find something wrong with Portland, move away from there, and probably be forced to move back in with her father for lack of money. He crushed the fantasy she had been living on, and in doing so, crushed her spirit. The combination of feeling depressed and angry made her mind like a blank slate, but not the kind of blank slate that is cultivated from years of practicing meditation. Rather, it was a dirty, worn down, gray slate that nothing good could come in or out of.

When she got to the house, she went straight into her room, closed the door and collapsed on the bed face down and still fully dressed. She had about seven hours of light sleep filled with a series of vivid dreams that played in her head like a reel of short horror films. She couldn't remember any coherent plot lines in her dreams, but she did recall that she was being chased by some monster that looked to be made out of clay and had a head like a giant turnip. She distinctly recalled a feeling of entrapment as she ran from the monster. No matter which way she turned or how fast she ran, she couldn't get away. The only way out was to wake up, and so finally she screamed herself awake.

༶

Cosmo waited a few days to send an apology email to Silvia, and although the word "sorry" didn't appear in the letter, she knew that it was the closest thing to an apology she would get from him. There was a link to an article from the *New York Times* about Portland declaring that it was a super place to live. Silvia wrote back to corroborate what the article said, and to ask Cosmo if he would consider moving there with her. She offered many reasons that moving to

Portland would be good for him: Anything he was doing in Philadelphia, he could easily do in Portland; Portland is much nicer than Philadelphia and has nearly the same cost of living; Portland has the best public transportation system in the country, and as Cosmo didn't own a car, it would be perfect for him; and last but not least, there are lots of cute hipster girls in Portland! He responded by saying that, despite her viable arguments, he still didn't see any compelling reason why he should move to Portland and added that he hated hipsters.

She would have written back with more attempts at persuasion, but she knew that her attempts would be futile. She knew that Cosmo was born content and that he could be content no matter where he lived, because place wasn't important to him. She admired and resented him at the same time. He didn't need to get away. He never even went on vacation and he would never get excited about their one family vacation to Montreal every year in August, whereas she had thought of nothing else but Montreal all summer.

Even more, he seemed to have a permanent sense of space and freedom, as if he could be on the other side of the world without leaving his apartment. Silvia always felt as if her world was closing in on her, regardless of the distances she traveled or the openness of the space around her. She did have her painting, which worked well to free her spirit, but in the absence of her art, she was trapped in her thoughts about place. She thought about her current place, how she wanted to get out of there, and where she would move next. She wondered why her own brother had this sense of permanent freedom and why it was so hard for her to be free. They were two very different people and both responded to their worlds in two entirely different ways. Cosmo never seemed to be too bothered by Frank's yelling. It just boomeranged off of him. But their father's screams penetrated Silvia's skin and went right into the very core of her being.

For a long time, Silvia just accepted Frank's rage as something that would take too much energy and strength to change or alter in any way. But now she thought, if he sobered up, he might be less raging. He might even be less inclined to ruin the upcoming family gathering, as he had ruined so many in the past. Although she knew that he would probably not be able to get sober by the date of the gathering, she did think that, at least, he could get started on the path to sobriety. She didn't stop to consider the great magnitude of such a challenge, or that such a thing may not be possible. The only trick for her was to figure out *how* sobering Frank up would be possible. She knew she had to get him to an Alcoholics Anonymous meeting and she called Angie in an attempt to persuade him.

"Dad's not going to go for that Silv. You know that," Angie told Silvia over the phone. Silvia could hear Angie's little daughter, Isabella, crying in the background so she said goodbye to her sister, who seemed as if she was not able to help anyway.

After hanging up with Angie, she considered calling her Uncle Nick who had several years of sobriety under his belt and had been attending meetings for many years. Silvia knew all about his struggles with alcohol, as he wasn't at all shy about talking about his plight from a falling apart drunk to a sturdy, sober man.

Uncle Nick was Frank's older brother; shorter and stouter than Frank, with a big head of hair in a black pompadour and a slight widow's peak in the center of his forehead. When Cosmo was young, he nicknamed him Eddie Munster because of his hair, and the Greco children would secretly laugh behind his back. But they all loved him. He was a lovable sort of guy that came to their house every Christmas dressed up as Santa Claus, with lots of hugs and toys for all of them.

Frank liked Nick. Even more, he respected him, which was much more than he could say for his other brother, Paul, of whom he didn't think very much. Paul was so obviously favored by Frank's mother, and because of this favoritism, the two other brothers resented him bitterly. They also resented his success as a partner in one of Philadelphia's premiere law firms and his seemingly functional family. Most of all, they resented his ability to sip a martini at a formal dinner party with friends in his antique-filled Main Line house, without needing to indulge in a second, third, fourth, fifth, and so on. But there was something else that made Frank and Nick dislike Paul so strongly. He hid behind the façade of a nice guy. He had a cheerful, bright disposition and appeared to be a great, easy going and genuine person, but he was a fraud. Even though Silvia had often wished for a different father, she was grateful for not getting her Uncle Paul for one. Her father was crass and crazy and scary and mean, but at least he was honest. With Frank, you knew what you were getting.

Because Frank and Nick had this mutual enemy and no other siblings, they were closely bonded and influenced each other. So when Silvia called her uncle to tell him that she was sure that her father was an alcoholic, and sure that Donna left him because of it, Nick wasted no time in calling his brother and convincing him that going to a meeting was the only way he was ever going to be able to quit drinking. But both Silvia and her uncle failed to recognize one very crucial nugget of information: Frank didn't want to quit. He didn't have a problem with his drinking. Everyone else did. But he went along with the whole meeting thing to appease his brother and quite possibly to make his persistent daughter relent a little.

Silvia got the day and time of the meeting and told Frank various times throughout the week that they would be going to the Wednesday night meeting at seven o'clock. She also left a note on the kitchen table on the morning of the meeting. Even though she knew that there was no way he could have forgotten, he pretended that their plans slipped his mind, and when she came home at 6:30 in the evening, she found him sitting in the kitchen having a drink.

"Dad!" she snapped as he was taking a sip from his glass. "You know we're going to that meeting tonight!"

"Oh, I forgot," he said with a smirk that made it obvious to Silvia that he was lying. "Well, just wait until I finish this drink, and we'll go."

Silvia knew that he didn't expect her to take him up on the offer to go to the meeting after having a drink, so he seemed surprised when she came back from her room in a change of clothes and told him that she was all ready to go. She drove, while Frank switched the radio. When he decided that there was nothing on the radio that he wanted to hear, he began whistling. He whistled loud and clear, making occasional trills. He was an excellent whistler, and Silvia always thought that if he had ever entered some sort of whistling contest, he would easily win. Whistling seemed like a happy-person thing to do, so she wondered why he whistled. Maybe there was a part of him that wanted to be happy, that wanted to break free from his shell of misery, and whistling was how he tried to do it.

❧

The meeting was held in a room in the back of a local church, with dim lighting and a bunch of rat colored folding chairs formed in a circle. It was the same room where old people played bingo on Friday nights, where the young kids had their catechism classes on Sunday mornings, and where the drunks came to get sober on various nights throughout the week. With a group of well over fifty people, Silvia assumed that she picked a popular meeting. There were a few formalities in the beginning, including an opportunity for any newcomers to announce to the group that he or she had never before attended a meeting, at which time, Frank elected to stay silent.

Silvia had no expectations of him speaking up. She knew that, as far as he was concerned, he should not even be at this meeting. He wasn't an alcoholic. He was just someone who liked to have a good time. He would not have come to the meeting had it not been for his desire to please his *good* brother. Frank claimed to be an extrovert, needing to have people constantly around him, which went along with his *choice* to drink. He was a highly sociable person who liked to have fun, and Silvia was an introverted weirdo who could stay by herself painting happily for hours. Her diagnosis of him as an alcoholic was also due to her own abnormality, which was undoubtedly the fault of Donna's bad genes. She could sense Frank sitting there next to her as an observer, not a participant of this group of defective people to which he didn't belong. But at least he was there.

A few people spoke for only a few minutes each giving brief updates of their week. One man was having a very bad week.

"A huge tree fell on my car this week," said the man through his big seventies mustache. "Lucky I wasn't in it. But maybe it would have been better if I had been in it. I got pink slipped this week at work, and my ex is bringing me back to court to get an extension on her alimony."

A skinny woman with dark, almost black, lipstick, spoke up in a cigarette voice. In addition to her bad week involving a cheating boyfriend, it seemed that her entire life consisted of nothing but problems. She spoke quickly as if to squeeze all of her problems into the short amount of time that she was given to share. Most of what she said was an indecipherable blur with certain select phrases like "cheating-no-good-mother-fucker" and "some-crazy-bitch-at-work" popping out. The poor lady had been to three other meetings this week alone, including Narcotics Anonymous, Adult Children of Alcoholics, and Love and Sex Addicts Anonymous.

Next, a guy who looked like an over-aged high school burnout, talked briefly about how he had recently traded in his addiction to pot, or as he called it, his TCH maintenance, for drinking. He never liked the taste of alcohol too much, so he figured it would not be so dangerously addictive for him, but he was wrong.

"And before I knew it, I was a boozer," he said with the laugh of a simpleton.

Next, a very hunched over tall lady spoke. As she spoke, her eyes grew big and filled with fire. "I'm feeling like I'm going to do something scary. Really scary. I don't know what it is yet." Her hands were shaking, and she was moving back and forth in her seat, making her stringy hair move through the air like strands of hay blowing in the wind.

After each person spoke, no matter how grave or sad or lighthearted their story was, no one else in the group commented. They all just sat there listening with blank faces and stiff bodies. They remained this way for the entire duration of the main speaker's long sad story, which lasted for about a half an hour. The speaker was a thin, older man with white hair, a face full of worry lines, and a navy blue suit that looked as worn out as the rest of him. His tired eyes and broken smile spoke loud and clear of the many hardships through which he had stumbled. But not as loud and clear as his story that had a marked similarity to Silvia's story. Despite the man's soft-spoken voice, his words blasted in her ears. This man had her same proclivity to move from state to state and city to city, and he referred to himself as a "geographic." With each move, he had conveniently erased his past mistakes only to make new ones. He stopped moving once he got sober, but sobriety took years. Meanwhile, he lived in denial of his alcoholism and his inability to stay in one place. Each new place was more than a clean slate. It was an opportunity to be a new person. A person who might magically lose his desire to drink. A person without pain.

Silvia was sitting forward with her shoulders back and her head straight up, as she listened intently to the speaker. He too had grown up in a household with a drunk for a parent. His mother started drinking when his father left her and their three children for a shot as a film star in Hollywood. As her drinking progressed, so did her erratic behavior towards her children, who didn't know what to expect from her and, eventually, from the world. They remained in a constant state of fear, always on guard. The speaker grew to hate his home and left it as soon as he could at the age of eighteen. He wanted to get as far away as he could, but he had very little money, so he hitchhiked to Los Angeles. He said that he may have secretly wanted to find his dad, but that he had never found him. Instead, he found a group of free loving acidheads who encouraged him to come with them up to San Francisco. "And that's when it all started," he said, as if he was exhausted merely by the act of talking about his past.

There began his twenty-year career of drugging, drinking, and moving. He started over more times than he could remember. He lived in twenty-five different cities in ten different states, many of which he had moved back to repeatedly. Every move brought with it a set of high hopes, which he knew, somewhere in the back of his head, would soon be shattered. With each new move, he drank more and more, and quitting seemed more and more hopeless. Eventually he gave up on trying to quit, and one night, he ended up passed out on a sidewalk in the lower east side of New York, where he had just moved back to for the third time. It was on this night that some homeless guy stabbed him in his right leg. "I thought I knew what *bottom* was until then. This was truly bottom, though," he said. He was rushed to a hospital, where his doctor urged him to join Alcoholics Anonymous. He took the doctor's advice and he had been sober ever since that night. His move to South Jersey in 1985 was his last.

Silvia felt that the speaker may have been there to warn her to change her ways or she too would be going down the same tragic trail. But her story could never possibly be that tragic. For one thing, she wasn't an alcoholic and had no intention of becoming one. For another thing, this move to Portland would very well be her last move. And her habit of moving wasn't a compulsion. It was bohemian. Gypsy. It was just something that she needed to get out of her system. It was just a coincidence that both the speaker and Silvia grew up in alcoholic households, and grew into people who liked to move from place to place on a very frequent basis. She would not end up as some broken down person telling a room full of people about her regrets and mistakes and how AA had saved her life.

Frank wanted to leave right after the meeting had finished, and Silvia, feeling weak from trying to differentiate herself from the speaker and convince herself that she would not end up anything like him, didn't have the energy to make her father stay and try to socialize with the others. She wanted to get out of there herself, away from the speaker, away from the doomed version of what she might become.

❧

Frank insisted on driving home and stopping off at a local diner that was inconveniently positioned on a traffic circle. It was a big, shiny, chrome-covered rectangle filled with red vinyl booths and a counter that stretched almost the entire length of the place. They ordered garlic fries and milkshakes. When the waitress asked if Frank wanted anything to drink, Silvia just glared at him, forcing him to tell the waitress that he would just have water. Silvia went to use the restroom. By the time she got back, the waitress had brought their milkshakes, and Frank had nearly finished his.

"I hate it when it's over," said Frank, taking the final sip of his malted shake.

On extremely rare occasions, Silvia felt connected to Frank, and this was one of those rare occasions. He was like a big, overgrown boy saddened by the ending of a milkshake. She even offered him some of hers because she knew that, despite his intense craving for more, he was too cheap to buy another. He was simple and innocent at that moment, and his eyes turned young. She had trouble comprehending how this harmless, youthful creature could coexist in the same body with the scary, old man that was Frank. It seemed as if whenever any good tried to glimmer through, the stronger more powerful side of his being would crush it.

She remembered back to the time that she got the scholarship to art school, and how proud he was of her achievement. "You're going to be the next Botticelli!" he told her with a smile so big that it looked almost painful. At first she thought his elation was due to his being off the hook of having to pay her tuition. But it was more than just his sense of frugality. He really was proud, and Silvia felt his approval shining down on her for the first and only time in her life. It was, however, a very short-lived period of time, as she suspected it would be, and soon Frank was back to his typical way of being in the world. Silvia came home one day to find her belongings out on the front porch, and upon going inside, she saw a note on the table that said that she had to leave the house immediately. Donna was away at a conference for work, so she couldn't intercede, as she usually did on her children's behalf. Silvia wondered what she could have done to upset Frank, but she also knew that her wondering was useless because it was almost impossible to know such a thing. What might upset him was anybody's guess. Maybe he was upset that she, like all of his other children, wasn't following in his footsteps and studying law or studying something like philosophy that would prepare her for law school. He was as unpredictable and volatile as a volcano. She also knew that, whatever eruption was happening inside of him, would soon settle down, and so she gathered her belongings on the front porch and went to a friend's house for the night.

"So what did you think of the meeting?" she asked him. His face turned from remorse, for finishing both his and her shakes, to suspicion.

"Why are you so interested in getting me to an AA meeting all of a sudden? Did Mom put you up to this?" he said.

"Oh what the fuck Dad! Can't a daughter take some interest in her father's well-being?" she said as she gathered bits of garlic and placed them on a fry.

"Watch your language."

"What about you? You curse all the time."

"That's different. I'm old. It doesn't matter that I curse." He looked down sadly again at his remaining couple drops of milkshake.

"So, you still haven't answered my question," she said, disregarding his warning about the use of profanities.

"It was pretty much what I expected." His face looked jaded. And then, in an effort to take himself out of the discussion, he said, "Boy, that speaker had some story, huh?"

"Well, how did you feel about being there?" she said, with an emphasis on the word *you*.

"Alright, I guess," he said as if her question made no sense.

"Did you get anything out of it?"

"What do you mean by that?" He squished up his face like a prune.

"Could you relate to any of the other little stories or the big story?"

"Not really."

"So, what's the chance of us going back next Wednesday?" She said this mustering up as much hopefulness as she could in her face.

"I don't really see the need for it. Look at that one woman with all the problems. The one with the dark lipstick. She goes to meetings all the time, and they don't seem to be doing her any good. In fact, they could be making her worse." Then he said he had to go to the bathroom and left without giving his daughter a chance to respond. As soon as he came back, she said, "I doubt the meetings are making her worse," as if there had been no break in the conversation.

"Making who worse?"

"Dark Lipstick," she said, making her father laugh at the nickname she had suddenly adopted for the woman from the meeting. His laughter was loud and mighty, like the rest of him. It made Silvia remember that he wasn't always miserable; that he liked to laugh; and that he had a good sense of humor when he wasn't busy being angry.

"Well, do you think you might go back, Dad?" she asked again, taking advantage of his current lighthearted state.

"Yeah, why not?"

Silvia accepted this reply and thought of her venture on this night as a great achievement. She was getting through to him when no one else could. She had a very quick miniature fantasy about him being a sober man, a good father, winning Donna back, and them all living peacefully ever after. She was quite proficient at fantasizing. Within twenty seconds, she was able to have a complete vision of what her family would become thanks to her amazing self. She saw Frank and her sitting in the living room with Vince and Cosmo and Angie. He was talking about how grateful he was to Silvia for saving him. He was calm and still and not his usual jumpy self, and he sat all the way back in his chair instead of on the edge. He was apologetic for not being a better father and was soliciting his children for ideas on how to get Donna back. Angie may have felt some slight jealousy towards Silvia for not being Frank's favorite for the first time in her life, but Silvia was, after all, the savior.

She would be the one to save Frank, and he was someone worth saving. He was, in fact, a great person in terms of his abilities and past achievements, and to have his greatness lost in a bottle of scotch was a terrible thing that affected not only himself and his family, but the world at large, as he was the type of person that had the potential to make a difference in the world. He wasn't the type of attorney that was just out to make a quick buck. He was the kind that was always on the side of the underdog– the old, the poor, the disabled– the most unfortunate people who had been wronged by the system and, therefore, by life. Even for clients not wrongly accused, he could look well beyond their rightful accusations and into the real cause of their wrongdoings.

He eventually became disillusioned with the system, after seeing one too many good people wronged by it. His disillusionment edged its way in through his spirit, little by little, until he turned into a broken man. The final culprit was an elderly client evicted from her apartment so that the new landlord could convert the building into condominiums. She was ruthlessly kicked out, and when Frank tried to fight for her rights, he was smashed by a system that was too big to fight. When he was asked to be a judge in his town's local courthouse, he accepted this honor with indifference. The part of him with hopes and dreams, the part that Vince had so strongly inherited, had faded out of him. Silvia could almost understand how something, like a lost dream, could drive a person drink.

But Donna claimed that it wasn't just a series of bad events that led to his alcoholism, but that he had been a drunk for most of this life. She thought that if he had had a different mother, he may have never been an alcoholic. But if he had a different mother, Silvia thought, he would not be who he was and, therefore, neither would she. Frank's mother was an angry woman with tremendous breasts and an intensely stern stare. She was calculating and clandestine and she spent her time spreading false rumors about her children in an effort to turn them against each other. She told Paul that Frank thought he was cheap, and told Frank the same thing about Paul. She told Nick that Frank didn't think much of him because he and his wife were childless, and told Frank that Nick thought his kids were spoiled brats.

By the time Silvia was old enough to have any recognition of anything, most of the damage in her father's family had already been done, and she only experienced the aftermath of the many wars that had taken place. For a short while, Paul lived in the same town as Frank, and when any member of one family would encounter a member of the other, they would just pretend that they didn't see each other. Frank's children were forbidden to speak with any of their Uncle Paul's children, so she had no opinion of her cousins because she didn't know them.

Silvia's memories of her Grandma Greco were mostly of her talking about dying, which, according to Frank, she had been doing since he was a small boy. She talked about it like it was a formal occasion, like a prom, a ball, or a wedding. She talked about her death as if it would be the end of everybody's world. She talked about it as if it was something she was looking forward to. But when her body actually got old, she held onto life like a vine clings to an old brick building, seeping her crinkled hands into the cracks of humanity.

She stayed in her house and saturated every nook and cranny with her crusty old smell. Silvia hated her house, which was dark and stale smelling and cluttered with useless, tasteless crap, like cheap ceramic figurines that looked as if they were purchased at the local dollar store. Silvia remembered being very disappointed when she found out that she and her family had to go to her house for Easter one year. Grandma Greco insisted on having the occasion at her house with her three sons and their children. Easter was her favorite holiday. Donna figured that this was because Easter had something to do with the long and painful suffering of Jesus. She relished her own suffering, as if she got the greatest joy from it. Grandma Tucci would call this "bella miseria," which meant beautiful misery.

Grandma Greco had palms hanging on the walls in her kitchen and her dining room. She made stuffed shells and a ham with pineapple. She bought Perogina chocolate eggs that were to be given out to the grandchildren. Unfortunately, there were not enough eggs for all of them.

"I didn't expect your family to come," she said to Frank in her shriveled up voice. "You didn't come last year or the year before." Frank could have responded back that they were not invited to her house for the past two years, but he didn't say anything. He respected her simply because she was his mother. Not only did he say nothing in his defense, but he also told his mother that she didn't need to give any chocolate to his children, and there they sat for the remainder of the feast, sad and chocolateless, gazing resentfully at their cousins. Uncle Nick went out after dinner and bought some Easter candy for Frank's kids as a form of compensation, but the old woman had nothing for them. Nor did she have any remorse or regret for buying less. Donna assumed it was intentional.

Silvia didn't hate anything short of the really evil stuff like Nazis and terrorists, but she came pretty close to hating her Grandma Greco. It wasn't so much for the way she had treated her and her siblings. It was how diligently and perseveringly she had damaged her father. According to Donna, she downright disliked Frank and disliked him even more after his motorcycle accident. What use could he be to her around the yard with that pathetic limp he developed as a result of the accident? Donna felt that Grandma Greco's feelings for her son may have come from the fact that he strongly resembled her own mother, who had chosen her as the least favorite of her four daughters.

Her husband, Silvia's grandfather, was a tall lanky man who looked like a tree that had grown crookedly. In the pictures that Silvia had seen, his hunched back and his forward leaning head made him look like he was always carrying a load of stuff on his shoulders. He died of a heart attack before Silvia was born. According to Donna, he smoked and drank heavily. "And with a wife like his, who wouldn't?" Donna would add. Silvia was relieved when her sinister grandma died, as she couldn't contaminate any more family gatherings, including Vince's graduation dinner. She thought that she would ask her father about this occasion tonight as he was in a decent mood.

"I think that we should do something to commemorate Vince's graduation," Silvia said in a nervous voice. "We can all go out to the Central Cafe or something."

"Are you serious? You know I'm going to end up paying for the whole thing if we do have something. You know I'm paying for his tuition and, for Christ sake, taxes are due in a couple of months!"

Silvia could have persisted, but she didn't. In fact, she didn't say another word on the subject. She had so few good times with her father, and she didn't want to spoil the good time that she was having with him now. So she kept her mouth shut and decided that she would re-approach the subject the very next time that he was in a bearable mood. She only hoped that that time would be soon, as Vince's graduation was around the corner.

CHAPTER 3
HOW TO BE FREE

When Silvia painted, she was free. Time didn't move forward, but swayed back and forth like a palm tree's branches blowing in a tropical breeze. This wasn't true of her other escapes, like music or movies. But through her own creation, she was afforded an opportunity to fly. She never thought of moving to a new place when she painted. She never thought of going anywhere. It was the only time when she was just where she wanted to be and when her mind was still rather than whirling about like a stick in a tornado. The more she painted, the less she noticed what was wrong with her surroundings and the less she thought about moving.

She used bright, cheerful colors and painted with big thick lines. Her world was inhabited by mythological beings, with human-like qualities, that lived in nature. Her fantastical universe was set against the strange and beautiful back drop of a place resembling the Sonoran desert, with big, black, mystery birds, giant saguaros that looked as if they should be growing on some other planet, and ocotillo trees with long, skinny branches reaching up as if they were trying to grab onto the sky. If Hieronymus Bosch was born a Mexican folk artist, his paintings might resemble Silvia's.

Painting real life was boring to Silvia, so she was surprised when she caught herself starting a self-portrait. She wanted to capture who she was beneath her skin. She wanted to convey the greatness of the spirit trapped inside her tiny body; how she was young and old at the same time; and how her mind wandered far and wide in an attempt to escape the confines of her skin. She made herself small enough to fit other stuff on her canvas, but wasn't sure what else she wanted to include in the painting.

She listened to the Beatles album *Revolver* as she painted herself. She always listened to music when she painted. Not the kind of music that bounced off her, but the kind of music that penetrated her skin and touched every cell of her being. Her taste was eclectic– everything from rock to folk to psychedelic. The music seemed to go right through her and ended up, somehow, on the canvas. If you stared at any of her paintings long enough, you could hear guitars, harmonicas and even the occasional wah-wah peddle.

She had been invited to join in gallery receptions and even had a couple of her own. But she steered away from the more elitist galleries, as she thought art was for everyone, not just the wealthy and affluent. She participated in making public murals, and even did some of her own street art on the sneak. Even though Frank didn't fully appreciate her work, he knew that other people did appreciate it, and he thought that she was foolish by choosing not to capitalize on her talents.

Maybe he was right, she was thinking on this particular rainy day. And maybe, if she had listened to him, she would not be driving to a nearby shopping mall in search of a job and thinking how lucky she would be, due to the current economy, to find one at all. Shopping malls were no by means one of her favorite places, and it depressed her to look for a job at one. At this time, she felt that she didn't have a lot of options besides the mall.

She tried, unsuccessfully, to tell herself that malls were really not that bad. They were just so completely insulated that they reminded her of Biosphere 2 or some other weird science fiction experiment, and made her feel claustrophobic. The excess of merchandise everywhere had a reverse effect upon her by not only making her not want to shop, but by making her never want to own anything for the rest of her life. The constant low grade noise that pervaded the air made her weak and dizzy. The other shoppers walking casually, as if they were enjoying themselves, made her feel alien because she couldn't relate to their ability to derive pleasure from this environment.

Despite her negative feelings towards the mall, she needed a job. Her fear of being stuck in her father's house, had already come true, and now she feared having to stay there for an indefinite period of time. She knew that the way out required money. She was ready and willing to do whatever necessary to make money, so that she could move far away.

She dressed in her most conservative looking attire, which consisted of plain black cotton pants and a plain white button down shirt– the same outfit she had worn at a previous banquet server job. Her hair was evenly and freshly colored dark brown and pulled back in a big, slick, black barrette. Copies of her resume were in hand, showing all of her work experience. She listed only jobs that she had left in good standing, which eliminated most of the jobs at which she had worked. She had listed in reverse chronological order: A natural food market in Tucson, a pottery store in Philadelphia, a used bookstore in Chicago, and an art supply store in Brooklyn.

Although she had a problem keeping a job, she never had a problem finding one. She didn't need the lure of a "Help Wanted" sign to walk into a shop and ask if help was needed, and for her proactive approach, she was often rewarded. But on this particular day, she tried nearly thirty shops with nothing but negative responses. She was ready to go for her second Cinnabon when she noticed a candy store that appeared to be new to the mall.

It was called, Savor the Flavor, and was filled with big, plastic bins containing a rainbow of bright, artificially colored candy. It had everything from gummy worms to candy corn to yogurt coated malt balls to chocolate covered raisins. The place was crammed with shoppers loading up little white paper bags with candy and taking them to the register. The cashier looked overwhelmed and jaded at the same time and wore an electric green apron that matched the rest of the store. Silvia was reluctant to ask her if help was needed because of the very uninviting expression on her face, but approached the girl none-the-less. The girl, in turn, called out to a man named James, who came through a door in the back of the store wearing a maroon suit jacket. He was tall and thin and stiff and moved like a life-sized wooden puppet. He was either the owner or the manager.

"Hello," Silvia greeted him professionally, "I was wondering if you are looking for help."

Grace Mattioli

"As a matter of fact, we are looking for a store manager. What kind of experience do you have?" He was curt and to the point, and Silvia liked that in a person. She took her resume out and handed it to him. He took one look at her resume and blurted out, "How do you live in all these places?"

She laughed, pretending to find this comment a humorous interpretation of her life, instead of the truth. She had a rich laugh that was just one more thing adding to her magnetism, and after hearing it for only a few seconds, he seemed to be impressed. Or at least impressed enough to want to do an interview with her on the spot.

"Let's go sit down and talk in the office," he said.

She had never had such an easy time making it to an interview and she anxiously followed him while rehearsing in her head what she would say to sell herself. He took her into the "office," which was little more than a broom closet jammed full of boxes of candy stacked on top of each other on some steel shelves.

They each sat on a couple of stools parked in the center of the room. When he asked her if she had any managing experience, she drew upon the few times that she had to train a new employee at her previous job at the natural foods market. She also talked about her opening and closing responsibilities at the art supply shop and how she was

84

solely responsible for the upkeep of the pottery store. She didn't mention the fact that the pottery store was the size of a large walk-in closet, and that, therefore, there wasn't much inventory for which to be responsible. Nor did she mention that the opening and closing responsibilities at the art supply store involved unlocking and locking the front door of the store. Rather, she embellished the duties of her past jobs. She also provided James with a brief description of the many qualities that would be sure to add greatly to the candy store's success. "I'm a fast learner, punctual, hard-working, and enthusiastic," she said, her eyes open wide, as if she had drunk too much coffee. Except for the fast learner thing, these were all lies, but she had the looks and the energy to make anyone believe that she did possess all of these qualities and more. James certainly seemed convinced. But convincing this stranger that she was here to stay would be much more difficult than convincing him that she would make a good candy store manager.

"I just purchased a mobile home only a few miles away from the mall," she told him. "So, I won't be going anywhere soon."

She surprised herself at coming up with this lie. It must have come from her experience driving past a mobile home development this morning on the way to the mall. Maybe, while driving by, she subconsciously was pondering what it would be like to live there. James looked back at her with a combination of credulity and admiration, undoubtedly for being so young to have purchased her own home. She knew that mobile homes were cheap, especially in today's crumbling real estate market, so this lie wasn't so far out of the realm of possibility.

He told her that he would give her a call after he checked her references, and he kept his promise. He called the next night to tell her that she was hired as the new store manager. She was scheduled every day from nine to six except Tuesday and Thursday. He told her about the other employees at the store. There was Dave who was diabetic, so "you don't have to worry about him stealing the candy." There was Connie, who was a senior in high school and worked the night shift, and did way too much socializing during her shift. "But you know how high school kids are," he added. The night manager was a kindergarten teacher named Alicia. He told her that he would meet her the next day at nine in the morning in front of the store.

She hung the phone up feeling proud of herself. She was almost embarrassed for feeling proud of her new mall job. But it was, never-the-less, an accomplishment. It was a management job. And it was in a candy store. It would be fun. When she thought of candy, she thought of her family's summer trips to Canada when she was always sure to get a big lollipop that had vibrant swirls that went around and around. She enjoyed looking at it even more than she enjoyed eating it. Cosmo would try to hypnotize her with it. Angie tried to steal it from her. And Vince just looked at it with curiosity and wonderment. There were no giant sized swirl lollipops at Savor the Flavor, but there was a plethora of other candy varieties. The next day when James met her at the store, he talked about all of the candy, but mostly about the gummy bears.

"They're your bread and butter," he said with a big grin, assuming she cared about the sales of the store as much as he did. "If the distributor ever tries to send you a box of blue whales after you've specified gummy bears on the order form, don't accept it!" he warned her. Then he went on about the blue whales as if he had something against them. "They just sit there in the bins. They don't move."

Silvia couldn't imagine getting on the phone with anyone, demanding that they compensate for their blue whale mistake. She wondered how long James worked for the company before he began speaking in this strange candy language. Furthermore, she found it difficult to keep a straight face as she listened to a grown man talk so seriously and passionately about candy. But he was, after all, the vice president of the company. And to his credit, the company was doing well, even in these tough times. There were eleven other

Savor the Flavors spread throughout malls in Southern New Jersey and Eastern Pennsylvania. The store where Silvia now worked ranked pathetically low in sales at number ten, but she felt nothing for the cause of bringing up the sales. In fact, she was probably doing the locals a favor by keeping the sales low, thereby not contributing to the local population's obesity problem. Of course, she would not reveal a trace of her work ethic or her inherent laziness for this cause to James. As far as he was concerned, she was a shiny, young, ambitious recruit starved for learning the business of candy and eager to increase sales.

While James continued to talk, she half paid attention and half fantasized about moving to Portland, and as the minutes drifted on, his voice got so muffled, he came to sound like an adult in a Charlie Brown cartoon. Fantasizing would be the only way she would be able to endure the remainder of her orientation. She imagined herself clearly in the downtown of Portland with her friend, Emily. They were talking about something more meaningful to her than gummy bears and blue whales. She then saw herself riding her bike in the rain and going out to eat burritos with her new boyfriend. And of course, he was *the one*. She had searched high and low, but she had finally found *the one*. She then imagined herself at whatever job she could find there, and this is where the fantasy became most vague and even somewhat disturbing. She saw herself working in a mall job just like this one, and all of a sudden, James's speech became more clear and pronounced. It was actually a good time for her fantasy to go sour, as he was talking about the process for ordering.

"Orders are made every week," he said. "They're called into our main office in the city."

He showed her the process for ordering, and then it was about time for the store to open to the public. He turned on the store's fluorescent lights that made the candy shine so brightly that Silvia's eyes burnt for a quick second. Children were waiting anxiously at the doors, accompanied by their tired looking mothers seeking to appease their little ones with candy so that they could proceed with a day of shopping. Silvia had not had any experience with children, so they may as well have been really short aliens from another planet. She had never baby-sat, and because she and Angie had seen so little of each other in the past couple of years, she barely had an opportunity to hold her little toddler niece, Isabella, in her arms.

A small Asian girl with pig tails and overalls ran towards the coke bottle candy canister, opened the lid, and took out a piece of candy right as her mother came over to reprimand her. The mother then looked at Silvia and apologized for her daughter's misbehavior. Silvia wasn't used to being apologized to. Usually she was the one apologizing to someone for something. It felt good to be on the right side of the fence. She then felt a little tug on her shirt and looked down to see a little boy, with dark hair and big-rimmed glasses, who wanted to ask her something. It felt good to be bigger than someone for once.

"Hey lady," he said, his little face looking up at her, eyes like saucers, "can you get me a lemon slice?"

"A lemon slice *please*," corrected his mother, who was standing behind him.

"Oh, yeah, please," said the little boy.

"Sure honey," she said realizing that James had forgotten to show her how to open the candy case where the fruit slices lived. He gladly showed her how to open the case and demonstrated how the fruit slices should be properly taken out with tongs and placed in the tiny paper bags used for candy from the case. He was business-like and efficient, but also had a sweetness about him. Silvia figured he had to be sweet to work in the candy business.

The morning flew by, and before she knew it, it was lunch-time. She forgot to bring her lunch, so she went down to the food court and bought the only thing that she could afford– a bowl of rice at the Chinese restaurant stand. After lunch, she went right back to the candy store without the usual dread she felt when returning to other jobs after a break. She thought it might be because she was working with a completely new group of people. Her lack of familiarity with children didn't make her uncomfortable. It made her curious. When she saw them entering the store with fresh, innocent faces, her own curiosity about them increased. To her great surprise, she was only slightly irritated by the whiners. Mostly, she found the children's spontaneity and their lack of conformity to social customs refreshing. They were free in their own simple way. Silvia attributed their ability to be free to the fact that they were too young to care how others perceived them. As she peered around the store, with kids running wild and bright candy colors, she started to feel like maybe this job would not be so bad. Maybe she would even eventually start to care about the difference between gummy bears and blue whales.

ॐ

Donna walked and moved through the world like she knew exactly where she was going and what she was doing at all times. She walked with a busy stride of self-importance that made her fit right into any big city, such as Philadelphia, perfectly. She was content in this city, and Silvia assumed that, like Cosmo, it was because she really had nothing else to compare it to. She approached her daughter, who was waiting for her on a bench in the New Market section of the city, appearing fresh and vital, dressed in a cranberry colored cotton dress. Her olive skin glowed like a freshly waxed apple, and her hair was pulled back to reveal the high cheekbones that Silvia wished she had inherited. Donna usually wore bland-colored clothing with a lopsided hairstyle. She usually looked downtrodden, tired and worn out. But today she was fresh and vital.

Only in recent years had Donna become worn down as a piece of old newspaper. She saw pictures of her mother as a young woman, shimmering bright and pretty with a full effortless smile and wide open eyes. Today she looked almost as good as she did in the old photos, and Silvia could only assume that her mother's renewal was due to the fact that Frank wasn't dragging her down. And although Silvia was glad to see her mother shining with vitality that could only be attributed to her being away from Frank, she was sad that Donna appeared to be moving away from her father and that the prospect of them getting back together seemed bleak. Her sadness confused her. She knew that Donna was much better off without Frank and that he was probably better off without her. Maybe now he would get himself together.

Silvia was dressed in her favorite style of sixties vintage clothing, with an orange mini skirt, a bright yellow top, and knee-high length, white boots. She looked like a 1968 sunflower. It was the first day in a long time that she felt like dressing in a happy outfit and the cheerful attire marked a symbolic end to her recent depression.

Donna suggested they go to dinner at a new restaurant conveniently located around the corner. It was called Charlotte's Place and was filled with dark brown wood, green leather chairs, and had warm dim lighting coming out of imitation Tiffany lampshades. The waiter came straight to the table with menus and a basket of bread and proceeded to mechanically pour water in their goblet shaped glasses. Silvia was astonished when her mother said that she was ready to order, without a several-minute study of the menu followed by questioning the waiter. In the past, Donna was plagued by various ailments that prevented her from eating just about everything. When Silvia was a child, Donna had chronic fatigue syndrome, which somehow led to her lactose intolerance. In more recent years, she decided that it wasn't chronic fatigue syndrome that had caused her constant state of exhaustion and lethargy, but something called Mediterranean anemia. It was no longer milk from which she needed to abstain. It was gluten.

"I'll have the turkey dinner and a glass of Chardonnay," she said with perfect clarity and decisiveness in her voice.

Fortunately, there was only one option for Silvia on this meaty menu, and so she was able to order pretty quickly as well. "I'll have the Portobello mushroom sandwich and a Perrier," she said without looking up from the menu.

As soon as the waiter left the table, Donna said, "So how are things going at home?"

"I got Dad to an AA meeting last week," said Silvia. Donna pursed her lips and opened her eyes wide as if astonished by her daughter's update.

"How did you do that? I tried many times and had no luck, so I just gave up on trying."

"I talked to Uncle Nick about it," said Silvia buttering a piece of bread.

"Why didn't I ever think of that?" Donna looked into the air as if the answer to her question would appear on the ceiling.

"It wasn't easy, though. I had to remind him every night before we went, and then on the night of the meeting, he acted like he forgot, and tried to get out of it. But I was persistent."

"That's wonderful, Silvie. How did Dad do?"

"Mostly he acted like he didn't belong there, like he was just going to please Uncle Nick. But at least he went. And when I asked him if he'd go again, he said he'd consider it.

Of course, I'm sure I'll have to persist again and I'm sure I'll have to go with him again."

"What made you think of getting him to a meeting, anyway?" said Donna while eating a piece of bread as if she had not, only a few months ago, proclaimed to the world that she would never again eat wheat. Silvia was reluctant to tell her mother her belief that Frank's drinking was the thing that fueled the continual feuding that existed within their family, and that she was going after this problem in hopes that they might be able to have a pleasant family gathering for Vince's graduation. So instead, she told Donna that it was just something that she thought would be worth a try.

She wasn't sure exactly why she was reluctant to tell her mother her theory of Frank's drinking as the root cause of all of their family fighting. Donna surely knew the truth of this theory. But, for some reason, she didn't want to remind her mother. She supposed that her reluctance had something to do with her secret hope that they would get back together, and this *could* happen if Frank was to transform in the way that Silvia imagined. She didn't have experience with anyone who had undergone such a radical transformation as the one that she was imagining for her father. She only knew of the fictional character, Ebenezer Scrooge, who had changed in this fashion. And that change took three ghosts, which was much more than some Alcoholics

Anonymous meetings. Maybe she should try to get him to a therapist. But she knew that her father would never agree to anything like that, especially because it would cost money.

Surely there was hope for Frank. Donna would not have married him if he were nothing more than an ill-tempered, unstable person when they met. Or would she have? Her own father, after all, was like an older version of Frank. He was charismatic, fun, and charming, like Frank, and used these parts of his personality to mask his monster side, also like Frank. Silvia could see how it was easy for her father, like her grandfather, to hide behind himself. To be dashing. To be the kind of man that women could fall for. He was a charmer. He always told Donna that she was beautiful. He showed up at least once a month with a bunch of flowers. He made a point of bringing her out to dinner every Friday night. Sure, the flowers, partially wilted, always appeared to be discounted, and the dinners out were sometimes at Wendy's or a local pizzeria. But it was the thought that counted.

In the many photographs of the couple when they first got together, Donna's face glimmered with the shine of being in love. "They made music together," Grandma Tucci told Silvia once. Silvia imagined them to be one of those electric, in-love couples that other couples looked at with a combination of envy and admiration, and that together, they were free. She thought that if only they could have stayed in love that they would have not broken apart, and then maybe all of the Greco's would coexist peacefully with each other, and planning a family gathering would be fun instead of difficult.

There were photographs of the couple dating back to the early eighties before any of the kids were born, before they were even married. There was a photo of them when they met in the summer of 1980 with the two of them on South Street in Philadelphia. Frank had his 'I Shot J.R.' T-shirt and Donna wore her hair permed and fluorescent pink lipstick. There was one of them at The Who concert in 1982 at JFK Stadium in Philadelphia, and one taken during the summer of 1981, when Frank won a stuffed bear at a shooting gallery on the Atlantic City Steel Pier. There was one of Frank's graduation from law school in 1983 and one of their long awaited wedding in 1984. Donna wore a blue velvet dress and Frank wore something that looked like it came from the Merry Go Round or one of those other mall shops so popular in the eighties.

She tried to remember when Frank changed from the guy in the photographs, looking happy, fun, and in love, to the miserable, angry person he was now. She tried to remember when her mother's face stopped shining and became dull, or when her eyes lost their brightness and started peering out into the world as if there was nothing to see. She tried to remember when her parents came apart and stopped being free.

Donna broke into Silvia's thoughts by asking if she had found a new job.

"I did find one, and at the mall of all places," said Silvia with slight embarrassment about working at the mall, as she had complained about it since she was a child.

"The mall, huh?" said Donna reservedly. "What kind of store?"

"A candy store. One of those bulk candy stores where customers fill up their own bags."

Donna gave her daughter a sympathetic smile, and Silvia, who hated sympathy, jumped back at her mother and said, "I feel lucky to find anything, Mom."

"You know it will only be temporary, honey. One day you'll find a career that will be truly rewarding. You're so smart and talented, Silvie." Despite Donna's attempts at bolstering her daughter's self-esteem, her compliments did little to restore Silvia's confidence. In addition, Silvia was caught off-guard, as she wasn't used to her mother being so supportive. Donna wasn't the most maternal mother. Cosmo thought it had something to do with her being sandwiched between two sisters with whom she never got along. Donna gravitated towards her four brothers, and in doing so, may have stripped away her more feminine qualities, including the maternal instinct that her children, especially Silvia, had so badly wanted in their mother.

"Oh my," said Donna in response to the huge plate of food the waiter set before her. "You have to help me, honey. I know you don't want the turkey, but maybe just some of the sides." Silvia gladly accepted the offer and took a generous amount of stuffing, mash potatoes, and cranberry sauce.

Like most people, Silvia associated turkey dinners with Thanksgiving and was reminded of the one when she was ten. The weather was unusually warm on that Thanksgiving Day, which put everyone, except for Frank, in a good mood. He had used the holidays as an excuse for drinking even more than usual. When Donna would try to caution him about having another drink, he'd blurt out, "It's the holidays for Christ sake!" On this particular day, he had prodigiously searched in every corner of the house for some kind of fight, and was gravely disappointed when he had found none. So when Cosmo showed up for dinner, stoned, Frank was relieved to find an excuse to fight. Donna telling him to "take it easy" propelled him into a state of rage that stayed fresh in Silvia's mind to this day. His quick, Incredible Hulk transformation was followed by a scream at Donna to "Fuck off!"

He screamed to Cosmo, "You no-good-for-nothing loser of a son! You'll never make anything out of yourself!" His arms were raised in the air, as if he was holding a giant rubber ball above his head as he yelled. But Cosmo just kept on eating. In fact, he was the only one eating. Frank's frenzied abuse just seemed to bounce off of him, as he shoved a continuous stream of food into his mouth. His lack of reaction caused Frank to get more upset, who then started throwing plates and glasses on the kitchen floor. After that, he started crying like an overgrown child, as if he was furious and remorseful at the same time.

When he went into the bathroom, Donna grabbed the kids, and they all made an escape. Silvia remembered piling into her mother's car and zooming down the driveway as if they had all just robbed a bank and were now making their getaway. She remembered Donna stopping at a Wawa to buy a pack of cigarettes, as soon as they were far enough away from the house, and how upset she felt seeing her mother reignite the habit she had worked so hard to quit. They drove until they reached a Motel 6 around Moorestown and settled for the night. As they all huddled together in the small, dark motel room, Silvia could feel the sense of relief they all shared. But relief was only one of the many emotions. There was also sadness, confusion, denial, and frustration. Cosmo was coming down from his high into what appeared to be a state of depression. Vince was too young and confused to have any awareness of what was really going on.

Angie switched channels on the television, while Silvia drew pictures in her sketch-book. Donna smoked outside and then came inside. She then went to sleep only to wake up screaming at around three in the morning. Silvia consoled Donna by telling her that "Everything will be alright." At first, Silvia felt strange to be acting like a mother to her own mother, but then it felt very natural. The next morning, she resumed being a child by playing on a swing set that was just outside the motel.

"I joined Netflix," Donna said, as she sipped her wine. "Already, my queue is so long. I hope I live long enough to watch everything on it."

Silvia chuckled, "I have a feeling you'll be around for a long time." She wanted to add something like, "Now that you left Dad," but she stopped herself. She didn't want to go further into family drama at the moment. Rather, she just wanted to enjoy her food while she could because she knew that, at any second, Donna would continue her pursuit of asking about herself or their family.

"Do you ever think about what you would like to do, eventually, in terms of a career?" asked Donna, eating a piece of turkey with cranberry sauce.

"All the time, Mom. It's just that I rule out every idea I come up with." She stopped eating as if the subject at hand had ruined her appetite.

"Tell me some of them," said Donna, who seemed to be delighted and relieved that her daughter was opening up to her.

"Well, I thought of becoming a college professor, like you but that's a long road, like I'm sure you know. I just don't know if I have it in me to go to school that long, and with the economy being such crap, getting a job like that would be tough. I'm not into the whole graphic design thing. I don't want to get stuck working for some advertising whore. And I thought of museum conservation, but I would have to go back to school for that, and it seems like it might be boring and I might not be able to get a job."

"What about being an art school teacher? I can see you working with children."

Silvia formerly dismissed this option with the excuse that she didn't like children, but she was learning, through her brief experience at Savor the Flavor, that she really did like them. This wasn't a bad idea at all.

"Yeah, I can really see you doing that," Donna continued. "You're so playful and spontaneous for starters. You're an amazing artist. I think it's something that might be rewarding and fun for you."

A smile of hopefulness came upon Silvia's face, as she thought of doing something besides the dead end jobs that she had been working since she graduated college. This would be something that she might actually enjoy, and something in which she would be able to utilize her talent as an artist.

"Now you might have to go back to school for a teacher's certification, but I'm sure that can't be too difficult," Donna said. "Maybe you can live at home."

This last suggestion didn't bode well with Silvia, and she swiftly jumped at her mother. "You can't live with Dad! What makes you think I can?"

"You're better at it than me. Look at the way you got him to AA. Besides, living with him *temporarily* is not the same as being married to him."

"That's true," said Silvia, her new found hope returning. Indeed, maybe living with him would not be so bad. Maybe he would get better. Maybe he would even stop drinking. She had not heard him vomiting in the bathroom in at least a week. That signaled a possible cutback in his alcohol consumption. Besides, she would barely be at the house between work and school. And it would be temporary. As soon as she was done getting her certification, she would be off to Portland. She felt overcome by exhilaration. The first thing she would do tonight would be to look into teacher certification programs in South Jersey. Then she would have to find out about the requirements, costs, and the length of such a program. Her thoughts raced. She was getting ahead of herself, her mind zooming in her maniac fit of excitement. Her mother, who must have somehow intuited her daughter's racing, brought her back by the gentle reminder that she was still very young and had plenty of time.

&

But Donna's attempt to calm her daughter down was in vain, and within five minutes after getting to her father's house, Silvia was online to look up schools and programs. She discovered, from doing a small amount of research, some rather disturbing news: That if she was to get her certification in one state, it may not be reciprocal with another state. This could severely limit her bohemian existence, which was frightening, but she also knew would be for her own good. Maybe it would be better to move to Portland now. There was an undergraduate certification program in Portland, as well as a graduate program in the field of education. But it made so much more sense, financially, for her to go to school while living at Frank's. But what if she got her certificate in New Jersey and then had to live in the state indefinitely. Her body froze with fright. Even the idea of living in the area for the next couple of years seemed like a prison sentence. She saw herself drooping to classes at some nearby commuter college, coming home to her father's house only to find him drunk and passed out or drunk and raging. This scenario had no boyfriends, no dates, and no friends.

Just as she was on this long, dark alley of life in South Jersey, she got an email from Emily telling her how much she loved the city and how she was sure that Silvia would feel the same way. She said that she was possibly falling in love with a guy and that she might be getting a job at a local art gallery. Silvia took this as a sign that someone above, her Grandma Tucci no doubt, was trying to tell her to move to Portland and to pursue an educational program there. So Silvia began researching programs in Portland. Between researching programs and thinking of where she might spend the next two years, all the while compulsively checking her email, she was up until two in the morning. And she was supposed to drive up to North Jersey to see Angie tomorrow. It would be a coffee-filled day.

The ride up the turnpike got progressively busier and more chaotic as Silvia drove to Angie's home in North Jersey. Drivers became increasingly aggressive, fighting through their steel encapsulations. Weaving, racing, and tailgating. The increase in traffic, as she drove north, was telling of the difference between north and South Jersey. But it wasn't just the increased speed of life and the density of population. There were other more subtle differences as well. In the south, lunch meat sandwiched inside of long rolls are called hoagies; in the north, they are called submarines or subs for short. In the south, the convenient stores are Wawa's. In the north, they are 7-Eleven's. South Jersey is like an extension of Philadelphia. They share the same accent and style, while North Jersey shares the sameness of New York. There is Philly Jersey and New York Jersey, with the latter assuming superiority to the former.

"They turn their noses up at us," Frank often complained of the way northerners treated the southerners. Maybe it was reminiscent of the way northern Italian folk treated their southern counterparts, and Frank, having his roots in southern Italy, didn't like this snobbery one bit.

He also didn't like the idea that his favorite child had relocated to North Jersey. He didn't even want her to go away to college at Rutgers, but he was certain that she would return home after her four years. In fact, everyone in the family thought that she would be happy to come back home. But Silvia knew that her beautiful sister would quickly be snatched up by some rich guy with a bright future. And she was, during her junior year.

Doug Rothchild had just completed the MBA program at Princeton and was guaranteed a position at Goldman Sachs. After only a few months of meeting Angie, he proposed at his parents' Christmas party right in front of his family and their esteemed friends. His parents were surprisingly accepting, despite her ethnic diversion from their long line of pure blue bloods. Their grand children's eyes would most likely be brown, and they might even inherit some fat gene that the Rothchilds surely suspected to be lurking in the Greco family.

Frank was panicked that, as the father of a bride marrying into a wealthy family, he would have to spend a major amount of money for an expensive wedding, but he also figured that he would be off the hook for life. At least Angie had the good sense to marry rich. He still wasn't going to go for some gala affair, so the wedding was nice, but small. He told his daughter to tell her future in-laws that she didn't want a lot of people at her wedding and that that sort of thing would make her nervous. This couldn't have been further from the truth. Angie would have absolutely loved a big bash with lots of people she didn't know or care about. Angie's soon-to-be mother in-law was less than pleased with the idea of a small wedding, but she was glad that it was held at a local fine dining establishment. Silvia more than appreciated the absence of a cheesy wedding band and liked the smallness of the wedding party, which consisted of herself and Doug's best friend, a former frat guy named Ray, who made Silvia feel like she was invisible.

While Frank was happy that Angie was marrying into money, the occasion was sad and disheartening because his favorite child was moving away from him. When Angie announced the plans to her family, Frank pretended to be overjoyed, but he was a bad actor and everyone, including Angie, could see the sadness coming through his eyes. Donna understood and accepted his sadness, for she knew how he had invested all of his hopes and dreams into the one and only child who really seemed connected to him.

So none of the Grecos were really surprised when he got inebriated at the wedding party and made a toast while drunk. Embarrassed and uncomfortable, but not surprised. The toast consisted of some slurs, followed by a long pause that led pathetically into tears. Angie's new mother-in-law, who could drink and drink and drink and yet remain perfectly composed, suddenly looked weak with shock, like she might pass out at any instant. Angie smiled to the small crowd, as though to apologize for her father's poor behavior, too ashamed to be touched by his tears.

She always did manage to conceal her feelings better than anyone in the family. This frustrated Donna because she couldn't determine her own daughter's state of mind.

Angie seemed to enjoy keeping her mother in the dark and at a distance. Angie and Donna never bonded, and Donna blamed herself for this failing. She attributed it to returning to graduate school for a master's in English literature to fulfill a life-long dream to be a college professor. She realized, by the time that Cosmo was born, that this way of thinking wasn't the best thing for her children. But it was too late for her and Angie, and the little girl gravitated towards her father, who reciprocated by making her his favorite.

Despite being Frank's favorite and despite her beauty and popularity at school, Angie seemed incapable of enjoying life. She was stuck inside of her flawless skin as though imprisoned by it, never able to break through. Never free. She hid her sadness well, as it wasn't apparent to anyone except for Silvia, who was always able to see right through fake laughter and fraudulent smiles. Her extra sensory gift was especially keen when it came to feeling the pain belonging to one of her own siblings, and she felt great empathy for Angie. Angie reciprocated Silvia's empathy by confiding in her. So, one night, when she swallowed too many pills, it was Silvia, and not Donna or Frank, whom she told. It was Silvia who picked up the phone and called 911 the instant Angie told her what she had done. And it was Silvia who stayed by her side in the ambulance. It was Silvia's face that was the first thing that Angie saw after she awoke on her hospital bed.

Silvia's quick response showed her strong sense of responsibility, supreme sensibility and composure under the gravest of circumstances. It was this act that substantiated her reputation within their family as the sensible one, the one who had her head screwed on straight, the one to ask for advice or support, and as the one who always had to appear held together, even when she was falling apart inside. It was also this event that forged an unbreakable bond between the two sisters. Angie knew that Silvia cared, and Silvia knew that Angie hurt. Despite the fact that the two sisters resided in two entirely different worlds, they loved each other in a way that only sisters can.

This difference was apparent as Silvia entered Angie's house. Her home was well hidden from street view, surrounded by big, billowy trees and a stately black iron gate that opened up into a driveway that was more like a small road. The yard resembled a botanical garden, groomed to perfection, although Frank might say that his yard was more perfect. The house was a huge, modern, and striking off-white structure that screamed of ostentation.

Angie was waiting for her sister on the porch of her house, which was as big as the apartment that Silvia had previously rented with her ex-boyfriend in Philadelphia. Her hair was tied back in a short, peppy ponytail, and she wore faded jeans and a T-shirt. Even dressed down, she looked like a fairy tale princess. Beside her sat two little, white Maltese dogs that stared out at Silvia with timid curiosity. When the two sisters hugged, the dogs' curiosity grew and they began to sniff Silvia, but kept an appropriate distance, like the very well-mannered dogs they were. They relished Silvia's gentle pets upon their little recently groomed heads.

Angie commented, "They just came from the beauty parlor. They had their nails all manicured and everything." Silvia smiled, but behind her smile, she tried to calculate how much money had been spent on the dogs' visit to the beauty parlor. She estimated it to be more than she had spent on all of her beauty treatments in the past two years.

"Where's Isabella?" asked Silvia.

"Sleeping, upstairs. The nanny is here too."

An immediate sense of space, openness, and sterility came upon Silvia as they entered the house, and she felt exposed, insecure, and most of all, cold. The complete lack of clutter also made the wrapped gift box on the table very prominent. The big box was undoubtedly for Silvia. Since Angie had married Doug, she was quite generous to her little sister, and her generosity always took the form of clothing or shoes. Silvia figured that this had something to do with her older sister's disapproval of the way that she dressed.

"That's all wrong," Angie would say when they were kids, looking down at six-year-old Silvia dressed in a green dress and purple stockings. "You have to wear colors that match, or at least compliment each other." Then she would open little Silvia's drawers and get out a pair of appropriately matching stockings, either white or black, for her to change into. As Silvia grew older, Angie could no longer tell her younger sister to change into something else. She could only suggest it through buying her new things to wear. Silvia didn't mind, but didn't give it too much attention either.

"Because I missed your birthday. Better late than never," said Angie referring to the gift.

"Thank you, Angie," said Silvia with a combination of gratitude and guilt, for she had not gotten Angie anything for her birthday. She seemed reluctant to open it, but Angie urged her by saying, "Go ahead. Open it!"

Silvia wasn't surprised when she saw the box was from J. Crew, but when she saw that it contained a leather jacket, she felt an awful sinking feeling in her stomach. She didn't wear leather, as she couldn't wear clothing that was made of animals that she imagined were brutally and needlessly killed. Even her shoes were made of canvas or of synthetic materials. Despite her anti-leather convictions, she couldn't possibly imagine telling her sister, who rarely smiled, and who was smiling big and bold at this moment, that she was against all leather. She had no idea what a leather jacket from J. Crew cost, but knew it was a lot of money, and although Angie could definitely afford it, it almost seemed too generous.

"God, Angie, I don't know what to say," said Silvia, still slightly shocked.

"Try it on!"

Silvia tried it on, only to be more disappointed because it fit her absolutely perfect. In fact, she looked fantastic in this jacket, like it had been made for her. Maybe she could wear it and make this one exception to her no-leather rule. After all, it wasn't like she had purchased it. It was a gift. It might even be rude and ungracious to not wear the jacket. She wondered how Cosmo might react if he saw her wearing it. Either he would think it was a fake or know it was a gift from Angie. His seeing the jacket would probably create more fuel for the fire that existed between him and Angie.

This split between them started when they were toddlers and they used to squabble over who got more ice cream in their little plastic bowls. But Silvia sometimes thought that their conflict may have started as soon as Cosmo was born. Angie, who had a tendency towards jealousy, must have somehow sensed that her baby brother would be getting more attention than she herself ever got from their mother. As children, they destroyed each other's toys. She barbecued some of his Dungeons and Dragons miniature figurines to get back at him for beheading her favorite Barbie doll. They refused to be seen together at school as adolescents because their two groups of friends were so different. Cosmo would often refuse to drive to school in the same car as Angie, so he ended up walking the two-mile walk to school. There was a very brief period of friendship between them during high school, when they would sneak into local bars together. That ended as soon as Angie was off to college and came home for her visits declaring herself an adult, a woman of the world, and looking down at her young, inexperienced siblings with blatant condescension. Of course, no one resented this treatment as much as Cosmo, who was closest to her in age.

From that point on, the line between them became thicker and their relationship grew as icy as a Siberian winter. When she got married, Cosmo brought a girl wearing a dress that appeared to be made from aluminum foil, had a shaved head, and sported a giant pentagram tattoo that covered the back of her neck. The whole family was sure that Angie would never forgive him for that stunt, but she did, and she showed her forgiveness by asking him to be the godfather of her child. Cosmo thanked, but declined based on his religious beliefs that were pretty much non-existent. That finalized the divide in their relationship for Angie, and despite Cosmo's supposed numerous attempts to contact her via email, she had not responded, and the two had not spoken a word to each other since the godfather invitation.

With that history, how could Silvia ask Angie to come to an event where Cosmos would be present? This would involve any kind of trickery and manipulation she could conjure. She first tried to appeal to Angie's sympathy for Vince by telling her how difficult Frank was being about helping him out with his tuition, and how it would be nice to show their support for their younger brother.

"So Mom and I thought it would be a nice idea to have a little party after his graduation ceremony," said Silvia as she sat down beside her sister.

"Well, that sounds nice, but why do I have to be there?" she asked.

"Because you're Dad's favorite, and you being there would just make him feel so much more comfortable. Besides, you know Vince would really appreciate having you there." She didn't reveal that her plan to coerce Frank to go was largely contingent upon Angie's presence at the affair.

Angie looked stubbornly at the floor as if hoping that if she looked long enough Silvia might stop bothering her about going to the dinner. So Silvia added something that she knew her sister couldn't resist– her need for keeping up appearances.

"How would it look if we were all there except for you? How do you think Mom would feel if you deprived her of an opportunity to see her *only* grandchild?"

"Alright already. I'll go. But do I have to bring Doug? I know Vince can't stand him."

Silvia was caught completely off guard because she wasn't at all aware that Angie knew about Vince's dislike for her husband. She had always taken Angie for being less perceptive and observant. So she did the only thing that she could think of doing– she lied.

"That's not true."

Angie just looked back at her with a snide look on her face as if to say, "Don't bullshit me." So once again Silvia used the appearance thing.

"Anyway, how would that look to everyone, if you show up without Doug? Dad might think that he doesn't like our family or something. And Doug might think that we don't like him."

"Well, I guess that's true."

Silvia couldn't believe it was this easy. She was starting to think of herself as a natural peacemaker. When she considered this, she smiled inside. But one of her not-so-nice internal voices told her that she might just be a manipulative liar instead of a natural peacemaker, making her internal smile turn sour. And then the two conflicting voices inside of her reconciled by agreeing that maybe she was just a combination of the two. Or maybe making peace sometimes necessitated the use of some mild deception and manipulation. And if those bad things are used to make something as great and worthy as peace, then maybe, in cases such as this one, they are not so bad.

Angie then added what Silvia knew would come up sooner or later. "You know I haven't spoken to Cosmo in over three years."

"Don't worry about Cosmo. He'll be fine. I promise."

Then to get her sister's mind redirected, she said, "Now let's go see if we can find Bruce Springsteen's house. Didn't you tell me you thought you might have discovered the street that it's on?" Angie's face lit up, and she jumped up out of her seat like a jack-in-the-box.

"I'll go tell the nanny," Angie said, running out of the room.

❧

They drove around the neighborhood for close to two hours before abandoning their search for the house that might belong to Bruce Springsteen. Angie probably would have continued searching longer if she had not needed to get home before the nanny had to leave. They drove up and down the same few streets several times, Angie inspecting each house before deciding that none looked like the kind of house in which he would live. When Silvia asked her how she knew what kind of house he would live in, Angie said that she didn't know, but she knew that it couldn't be any of the ones they had seen today. Silvia didn't want to tell Angie that she suspected his house was probably secluded and well hidden from street view. She didn't want to ruin the little bit of happiness that Angie seemed to derive from the prospect of finding his house. It was this very sort of thing that brought Angie to life; that turned her from a listless young woman who apathetically stared out at the world, from her three million dollar house, into a bubbly girl full of energy and curiosity.

While Silvia knew that she would soon droop back into a gloomy state, she didn't expect her slump so soon after they got home.

"I feel so tired," she said, as if she barely had energy to talk. "Would you mind watching Isabella while I sleep for a little?"

"I'd love to," said Silvia. "Oh, and I brought her some candy."

At this, Angie turned around sharply and said, "Don't let her see the candy until after dinner. And then, she can only have one or two pieces. She gets too hyper."

❦

She was very hyper already. She ran from one side of her room to the other, moving items from one place to another, resembling a toddler version of Frank running around in the kitchen. Her room was big, bright, and full of all sorts of toys. She didn't play with her toys in the same way that Silvia remembered playing with her toys as a child. She seemed much more interested in rearranging them than actually playing with them, and also liked showing off this skill to her aunt. She had a big smile on her face as she did her rearranging, and if she could talk, she might say, "Look what I can do! Isn't it great?"

She was a very happy toddler, indeed, and why shouldn't she be? She was extremely fortunate and privileged, belonging to a very wealthy family, being in perfect health, and having seemingly inherited Doug's cheerful disposition and Angie's looks. But it was something more than these things that made her happy, as she didn't have any concept of her wealth or looks or health. Her mind was pure and empty, not overcrowded with information and polluted with fears and regrets. She, unlike her mother, was free. She seemed content just to be, and Silvia felt a strong desire to be a part of the universe of simplicity and freedom that her niece inhabited.

Silvia could also see how very malleable this little person was, and she had a desire to help shape her. She wanted to fill her with good things. She wanted to show her how to draw, paint, and maybe even sculpt when she was a little bit older. But for the time being, it would be enough to show her how to make something simple, like a drawing of a cartoon-like sun, a tree, or a house. She looked around the room for a drawing pad, but found none. So she found a small box that contained a toy and took the lid off, revealing its plain cardboard underside. This would have to due as a surface. She always carried a pencil with her, which she took it out of her back pocket, and began drawing a picture of Isabella on the box. Even with a simple pencil and a piece of cardboard, Silvia's drawing was superb.

After about one minute, Isabella grew interested in her aunt's pursuit, and sat down next to her with the most curious eyes Silvia had ever seen. So she put the pencil in her niece's little hand, very gently held her hand around the pencil, and guided it along to make a simple drawing of a face consisting of a circle for a head, two almonds for eyes, a triangle for a nose, and a half circle for lips. They then made curls on the head of the person. When the drawing was complete, Isabella was overjoyed and ran to her bedroom door saying "Mama! Mama!" Her excitement was too much to contain and her shrill little screams woke her mother, who came into the room to see the drawing she had made.

"Oh, that's really nice Isabella!" Angie said looking down at her daughter. She then looked graciously at her sister, and told her that she would get her some real paper for them to draw on. Isabella and Silvia spent what was left of the afternoon drawing, while Angie lay on the floor next to them, half watching them and half sleeping. Around six, Angie asked Silvia what she wanted for dinner.

"Don't we have to wait for Doug to come home for dinner?" asked Silvia.

"He works really late. And goes in to work really early. Sometimes, he even sleeps over at his office. In fact, you probably won't even see him this visit. I only really spend time with him on the weekends." She said all of this like she was perfectly fine with being married to someone who was rarely around.

Silvia went back to thinking what she might want for dinner and recalled the time that Angie used American cheese to make eggplant Parmesan. So she told Angie to just make something simple, secretly hoping that her sister would suggest that they order out, but Angie insisted on cooking and proceeded to ask Silvia about her dietary requirements.

"I'm still vegetarian," said Silvia.

"So you still don't eat meat?" asked Angie.

"Or fowl or fish or eggs," said Silvia, hoping that her vegetarian diet might discourage her sister from wanting to cook.

"Jesus, what do you eat?"

Silvia laughed and told her sister, "It used to be worse. I was vegan for a year, and I had no dairy at all."

"That's crazy."

"Don't go through any fuss for me. Really, I can just have some bread and butter or something."

Angie stared back at her sister as if her suggestion was completely absurd. She then said that she knew just what to make, and went downstairs to the kitchen carrying Isabella and signaling for her sister to follow. Silvia fed Isabella baby food from a jar, while Angie cooked, and in less than an hour the two girls were eating pasta fazool that, to Silvia's surprise, was really good. It was even delicious. She was hesitant to ruin her wonderful eating experience by bringing up Cosmo's presence at the family gathering, but she knew she had to, at least, attempt to smooth things out between them before they saw each other. Not sure how to bring it up, she blurted out, "You know I bet Cosmo's nervous about seeing you."

"Well, he should be. I asked him to be the godfather of my daughter and he turned it down. And then he said some bullshit about being an atheist or something." She looked down at her spoonful of soup as if she was mad at it.

"Agnostic."

"What?"

"He's agnostic, not atheist."

"I don't know or care what the difference is. Him saying 'no' to accepting that *honor* had nothing to do with his beliefs."

"Well then, why do you think he said no?"

"Because he never liked me. That's why!"

"Angie, he loves you. You're his sister." Silvia stared so strongly into her sister's eyes that Angie had to look away.

"You can love someone and not like them," Angie said, still looking away from her sister.

"He's never given me any indication that he doesn't like you," Silvia lied. "And I believe he really didn't want to be Isabella's godfather because of his beliefs. And who knows? Maybe he thought that she would be better off with a god-father who would remember her birthday every year, and get her nice gifts, and you know, someone who could be there for her."

"Well then, he should have told me that."

"Yeah, but you know that's not his style," said Silvia, scooping the last bit of soup up from her bowl.

"Then he should have apologized to me."

"I thought he emailed you, and you never emailed him back."

"Well, he didn't apologize in any of those emails," she said indignantly.

"Again, that's just not his style. I've never gotten an apology from him for any of the times he was a jerk to me. You know most people don't even know how to say sorry. It's tough to say sorry."

Both girls stayed silent for close to a minute, allowing Silvia's last words to weigh heavily in the air and resonate with Angie, whose facial expression turned from one of indignation to one with a slight bit of understanding. Silvia said all that she could say in Cosmo's defense, and didn't mention him for rest of the night. The rest was up to Angie.

❧

The next morning, Angie woke Silvia at eight o'clock. After showering and having a simple breakfast of oat bran flakes and blueberries, she said goodbye. When she began to walk away from them and towards her car, Isabella began crying and reaching out. Silvia came back to her little niece to console her and to promise her that she would see her very soon. And indeed it would be soon. Vince's graduation was in a couple of weeks.

CHAPTER 4
TO KNOW PEACE

Silvia was disappointed, but not surprised when Frank didn't come home on the night she had planned for them to attend a meeting. She had given him several reminders of the meeting throughout the week. She told him in the mornings before she left for work; she left him notes taped to his bedroom door and sticky notes on the refrigerator; and left a voicemail on his phone. She thought that he most likely had remembered and purposefully avoided coming home so that he would not have to go. When Vince came home, he found his sister sitting, staring at the door with a blank face, like she was asleep and awake at the same time.

"Hey Silvia," he greeted his sister like he was trying to jar her out of her trance.

"Dad and I were supposed to go to an AA meeting tonight," she told him, her face as glum as a bankrupt merchant. Vince looked back at her with a combination of astonishment and cynicism and said, "Yeah right, you were going to get Dad to go to an AA meeting?"

She didn't tell him about the plan for his graduation party, which was the impetus for getting Frank to a meeting. She didn't tell him her strong belief that if Frank stopped drinking, they could all be in peace. Instead she said, "I just thought it might be a good idea."

"And it is," agreed Vince wholeheartedly. "A great idea, in fact. Just not sure of the feasibility of it."

Vince's response didn't seem to match his young and idealistic character. She wondered if her younger brother was suddenly becoming a realist. But rather than asking him about this apparent transformation, rather than trying to convince her brother of the possible feasibility of her cause, and rather than telling him of her success last week in getting Frank to attend a meeting, she just responded, "I thought it would be worth a try."

Vince patted his sister on the shoulder, as if to say that it was a good try, and then he suggested that they take advantage of their father not being home and make use the kitchen that Frank always monopolized.

Becoming alive at the suggestion, Silvia popped up from her chair and went to the kitchen cabinet. She got out a can of garbanzo beans, a box of rigatoni, olive oil and a garlic bulb. She was delighted to find a bunch of broccoli rabe in the refrigerator. Vince sat quietly at the table reading a library book, as she proceeded to cook in silence.

While they ate, she wanted to have some pleasant dinner conversation– nothing about their family, her moving away, or him going to college. She supposed that she could talk about gummy bears and blue whales, but that would probably be really boring for Vince.. She could ask him about what he learned at school today, but she assumed that it wasn't much considering that he was a high school senior with only about one week of school left. She then thought of asking him about the book that he was reading. He mentioned the title briefly, and then he went on about some insight he had while at the library getting the book.

"I thought about getting a fiction book because I always read nonfiction, so I started looking through some of the new fiction books, and you know what? They were all about the second World War."

Silvia knew what was coming.

"You know what I think? I think that the government is trying to make us all think that war is our natural state.

That way we won't want to speak out against it. We'll just blindly accept it."

"And the governmen' is in cahoots with the publishing industry?" said Silvia sarcastically.

"That's right!" said Vince, not noticing her sarcasm.

"Hey, speaking of war," she said, putting her hand over her forehead. "I saw Rafa the other day, and he was asking about you."

"Who's that? And what's he have to do with war?" Vince asked with a big question on his face.

"Somebody from the protests we used to go to. You remember, big head of kinky hair, always smiling, real friendly guy?"

"Oh yeah Rafa. He was a nice guy. How's he doing?" He had such a large fork full of food that Silvia thought he would not be able to get it into his mouth. But he did.

"He seemed good. He's become a carpenter of sorts, works at a bar by my old school, goes to Occupy rallies when he can." As she said this, she strategically gathered a couple of beans, some broccoli rabe, and two rigatonis on her fork.

"Yeah, I should try to make a rally before I go."

"I'm sure you'll have plenty of opportunity for protests and rallies in Berkeley." She didn't mean to mention Berkeley. She was trying to keep the conversation clean and free of any and all controversy. It just slipped out, and she hoped that her brother would not pay too much attention to it, but that wasn't the case. He stopped eating and looked down sullenly at his food. Silvia reacted to his sadness by offering advice, by trying to fix the problem at hand.

"Hey what about a scholarship, Vince? Have you thought of applying for one? It would be too late for this year, but there's always next year. Aren't you like number seven or something in your class? You got all A's in your classes for Christ sake."

At this suggestion, he looked even more discouraged.

"There's no money left in this country for things like education. It's all been used up for things like killing people, burning oil fields, missiles, and tanks. People, like Doug, are busy stealing..."

"C'mon Vince," she interrupted him, not wanting to hear one of his tirades against the country. "Dad will help you. I'm sure of it."

"And why are you so sure of it?"

This would have been the perfect opportunity to bring up the family gathering she was planning for him. She could tell him how she suspected that this event might put Frank in a good mood because of him being able to see Donna, and how his mood elevation could factor into his willingness to help with Vince's tuition. But she didn't take advantage of the moment. She was too tired. Tired from planning the reunion, tired from working her new job and planning for her move, and tired from trying to sober Frank up.

Her reluctance for bringing up the issue of the dinner party wasn't only due to her current state of fatigue. There was something more. They were having such a nice quiet dinner, despite Vince's mild irritation at her Berkeley remark and she didn't want to ruin the peacefulness. It was a rare thing, indeed, to have a meal, an hour, a minute, or even a second, when there wasn't an air of drama in this house. There was always the presence of a fight in some form. A fight could be happening, or it could be brewing, or the remains of a fight could be lingering. They moved in stages, like hurricanes, earthquakes, or most any sort of natural catastrophe. It felt a relief, but alien to Silvia, to be in her father's house, without the presence of drama and chaos.

She was slightly nervous that Frank might pop in at any second to ask them why they were not eating whatever "delicious" thing he had made and stored away in the refrigerator, or to inspect what Silvia had cooked and make some derogatory remark about it, like calling it rabbit food. But he never came home that night, and though Silvia thoroughly enjoyed having the house free of her father's abrasive presence, she couldn't help but be angry about his absence and curious about his whereabouts.

When he stumbled in at three in the morning, she was awake worrying. Yes, worrying about her father. What a strange concept. She knew that the situation should have been reversed. Either she or Vince could have been out partying and keeping the parent up with worry. This was an upside down world. This was all wrong! And so was the way that she came into the kitchen, with her arms crossed and her punishing eyes peering down at her drunk of a father, like a mother peering down at her unruly teenage son. He was lying face down on the kitchen floor like he was completely unable to make it any further than through the back door. He looked so pathetic lying on the floor. It was tough to believe that he had attended a prestigious law school, was a judge, a father of four, and a husband of a college professor. He was someone who was so hyper-vigilant about food waste, but when it came to wasting his own life, he had no problem.

☙

Not surprisingly, the image of Frank lying face down on the kitchen floor stayed with her all through the next day. She was glad that it was a short day at work and that her relief would be coming in early. As soon as she got out of the mall parking lot, she gassed up her car, got on the Garden

State Parkway, and drove south. She knew she was heading to one of the shore towns on the coast, but not sure which one. She could have stopped at Ventnor, but it was too close to Atlantic City, and she wanted to be nowhere near that frenzied casino energy. She could have stopped in Ocean City, one of the last dry towns left in the country. It was clean and easy, with a boardwalk that stretched for miles. Or Sea Isle City. But none were far enough. Not only did she want to be far away from Frank's house and the image of him lying on the kitchen floor; there was something else.

She felt hungry for the road. She felt that she wanted to drive and drive and drive. She wanted to remember, in her bones, that same feeling she had during all of her road trips. During all of these long distance driving adventures, she felt strong, especially because she had done most of them alone. She could change a tire on the side of the highway alone. She could set up a campsite alone. When it was raining or too cold to sleep outside, she could check into a motel alone. When she remembered her times on the road, she felt that strength within herself and really loved being who she was.

So she drove until she couldn't drive any further within the state of New Jersey. She went until she reached Cape May, the most southern point of the state and the only place in New Jersey where she could see an unobstructed view of the sunset. As she approached the town, she caught sight of a white heron with its little beak pointed up to the sky, its skinny legs dangling in the air, and its delicate angel wings spread free.

She drove over a bridge, entered into the town harbor, and followed the signs to the beach. It was a weekday before the busy summer season, so the quaint little Victorian house-filled city wasn't terribly crowded. She parked only a couple of blocks from the beach, and stopped by a pizza stand to grab a slice that she took with her to the boardwalk. She sat on a bench and ate, as seagulls gathered around her waiting for her to throw them a crumb. One brazen gull came and stood on the bench right beside her as if threatening to take her food away. It caused her to eat so quickly that she got indigestion. She walked the length of the boardwalk, which was short and quiet, relative to other boardwalks on the South Jersey coast. There were few shops, one of which sold chocolate covered strawberries that Silvia couldn't resist.

The shore brought back memories of being with Grandma Tucci. These memories were vague and beautiful and looked like an Impressionistic painting in her mind's eye. She remembered sitting on the beach with her in late summer with wet, salty breezes blowing gently while they ate lemon water ice. They didn't speak or need words. They were bound together like fingers crossed or shoe strings tied. Just listening to the music of the waves— rhythmic, constant, and forever. Silvia came to know peace through her grandma and their times together at the beach. If she had not experienced this sacred space, she might not crave it so much. But she did experience peace. She knew what it felt like in her bones, in her stomach, and in her head.

Because she knew peace, she knew war. She could sense when a fight was in the air, feel the aftermath of a fight, and surely knew when a fight was happening. She knew the looks and sounds of a fight only too well. She knew the hateful words thoughtlessly thrown into the air, as if they could be taken back one day, as if they could go backwards. She recalled all of the times that Frank called Cosmo a failure, until the word failure eventually became a part of Cosmo's skin. There was also pain over the absence of words, like the time that Frank told Vince that he loved him and Vince said nothing back. The one word that was never heard in the Greco household was the word sorry, because to say sorry would be to admit to being wrong. Grandma Tucci was only too willing to admit to being wrong because she knew that admitting to being wrong was how she could become a better person.

She knew that all of their family fights had some point of origin, with most continuing for so long that the origin was lost. Whatever the origin, Frank was either in the center of all of the family fights, or sometimes on the sidelines, cheering the players on. Silvia knew that he couldn't help himself. Fighting was what he knew. It was what he was raised on. According to Donna, there was never a second of peace in the household where he was raised by a drunk father and a drama queen mother. His childhood memories were filled with frequent visits from the town police, who were on a first name basis with his father. When his father wasn't busy raising hell, his mother was busy turning her children against each other and threatening to kill herself because she "couldn't take it anymore!"

Although Donna wasn't a fighter, she had grown up in a family of fighters, and so she gravitated towards what was familiar. Hence, her marriage to Frank made perfect sense. Silvia reflected on how Donna's family feuding escalated when her father died. Her well-off sister hired an attorney to contest their father's will, and in doing so, divided the family into two factions. The money that her sister would have gotten from their father's estate wasn't worth the legal fees, but she had to get that which she felt she was entitled. With the law involved, there was no hope of ever salvaging what they had as a family. "There are fights about money, and fights about everything else," Silvia once heard her Grandma Tucci tell Donna, as if she was prophesying what would happen to her family after her own husband's death.

She went on to say that fights about money are dirtier, uglier and messier than other fights.

Silvia suspected that her siblings were going in the same direction as her parents' families, and she wondered what they might potentially devolve into given further complications that were bound to come. Frank had enough money for his children to fight over once he was dead, and perhaps one of her siblings would get the law involved. Although Silvia couldn't imagine that happening, she was sure that Donna also had not foreseen what happened in her family. She then moved to thinking about other potential conflicts. Surely, Doug would not be the last spouse that wasn't liked by one or more of the other siblings. She could imagine whatever militant hippie chick Vince would one day marry, and how Angie would condescend upon her. The godfather fight between Angie and Cosmo couldn't be the last of this sort of thing to occur within their family. As Frank and Donna moved further away from each other, a divide in their family was bound to evolve, with Angie by Frank's side, and Vince by Donna's side, and Cosmo and Silvia left floating somewhere in between.

For the first time in her life, Silvia felt the bigness of her family's feuding. It had a life of its own, with roots going back to the early nineteen hundreds, when one of Frank's great aunts caught her sister sleeping with her husband in their Naples apartment, or when one of Donna's great grandfathers ran through the streets of Milan chasing his brother for stealing his money. Would this continue into the future? She couldn't see a beginning or an end. It was way beyond some Alcoholics Anonymous meetings, or a family get-together. There was too much that couldn't be undone.

Many fighting scenes of her childhood passed before Silvia's eyes. She remembered, too, how, she would retreat to the cellar steps and dream about going somewhere far away. She had never been to a far-away place but had seen pictures of such places on the television and on the computer. One of those places was Paris. She imagined that she lived in a charming, bright, colorful studio apartment with a black and white cat. She also lived in a white cottage with red trim that was surrounded by chickens and sheep and situated in the pristine English countryside. Sometimes she lived in a weathered beach house on the California coast. As she got older and realized that living at any of these wonderful residencies depended on her having money, she imagined a career for herself. When she lived in the country or at the beach side, she made a living as a painter. When she lived in Paris, she managed an art gallery. She was famous in all of these communities, and everyone loved her and wanted to know her. And so it went. She could still hear her Grandma Tucci saying to her, "Sometimes dreams can hurt you." The wise old woman must have known that her granddaughter had an overly active dream life. But Silvia couldn't help herself. She was born a dreamer.

When old enough to move on her own, she traded moving in her head for moving in the real world. She looked down upon her father's restlessness and inability to stop searching for a lost frying pan. But how was she so different? She searched for happiness in places the way that Frank searched for it in a bottle of gin.

As she sat eating her chocolate covered strawberries, looking out onto the sea, and listening to the waves on this perfect late spring early evening, she wondered how she could feel such a strong and urgent need to move, to start over. She heard the words of the man at the AA meeting, who called himself a geographic, talking about how many times he had started over. She heard Cosmo saying, "What's wrong with here?" Indeed, what was wrong with here? She was hard pressed to find anything wrong with her surroundings or anything wrong with this day, short of the mooching seagull. Why was the next place always better than the present one?

As the sun was setting, she kept her eyes on it, not wanting to miss any of its very quick show. Once the sun touched the ocean, it would sink fast into the horizon. The ramble in her brain quieted down, as the big yellow ball slid down behind the ocean. At that moment, she realized that making peace in her family wasn't only for her parents and siblings. It was for her sake, as well. As the sun made its final decent into the ocean, she felt a new energy for her cause to reunite her family come alive. She now felt more determined than ever to make the family gathering happen. She firmly believed, if all of her family members could be in the same room and see into each other's eyes, they would remember that they loved each other. Then there would be an unprecedented peace in her family. She understood now why she was putting so much effort into planning the gathering and was so easily willing to prey upon her family members' weaknesses. This was underhanded and manipulative, but it was for the good of all. If there was some peace in her family, maybe there would be some peace in herself, and she could stop running.

She stayed in Cape May until nighttime when the outdoor mall lit up and was filled with people enjoying the lovely mild evening. The mall was on a cobblestone street and filled with cafes, pubs, and shops selling ice cream, fudge, and seashell souvenirs. With no cars on the street, Silvia didn't have to hear the roar of motors, beeping horns, and drivers yelling. The car-free aspect made it an especially pleasant place to walk and window shop. She strolled by a restaurant with outdoor seating where a tall, dark, curly haired waiter smiled at her. She smiled back, but then started walking fast. Immediately, she regretted not doing more and wished that she had gone up and talked to him. Flirting wasn't something that ever came natural to her, and it was only very recently that she acquired the skill of flirting at all. While in college, it was all too easy to meet guys, so she never had to worry about doing anything like approaching a strange man and conversing with him.

She wondered if she should go back to the restaurant where she saw the waiter and attempt to talk to him. It was too late now. Besides, she would be moving to Portland soon. More than that, she just felt stupid going back to talk to him, so she just continued walking on, feeling regretful and relieved at the same time. Then something inside of her made her turn around and walk back to the restaurant. To her dismay, the waiter was nowhere to be seen, and it looked like the restaurant might be closing.

"Just as well," she thought to herself. She got back on the road heading home and soon after got a call from Donna. "What are you doing driving down to Cape May by yourself at night? What if something happens, like a blow out?

You'll be stranded on the side of the road alone." She could hear her mother's panic through the phone.

"I'm sorry Mom. Don't worry. I'll be home soon." Donna had no idea of all the nighttime driving Silvia did alone and Silvia made sure that she never would.

"I want you to call me as soon as you get home," said Donna in her most firm tone of voice.

❧

Silvia did call her mother as soon as she pulled into the driveway of her father's house and she was sorry to find that Donna wasn't in the best of moods. "How's your dad?" Donna asked her right away, not even asking how Silvia was.

"Not so great. The other night...." began Silvia, who was then abruptly cut off by Donna saying, "Well, a bottle of booze a day can't do much for any body's well-being," as if she had had this statement all prepared and was glad that he wasn't so well.

"He doesn't drink a bottle of booze a day," said Silvia, surprised to hear herself defending Frank.

"Sorry, I should have said a bottle of booze every two days," said Donna sarcastically. She was detaching from Frank. It came through loud and clear in her voice, in her sardonic remark, and the way she was suddenly calling him "your dad" instead of "Dad." Silvia was both glad and sad at the same time. She was glad for Donna's newfound independence, but saddened that the fantasy she had about her parents' getting back together would probably not become a reality. Whatever mixed feelings she had inside, she didn't have the energy to defend her father anymore, so, instead, she asked Donna how she was doing.

"Fine," she replied, but didn't then speak of any other details, as if she didn't want to disclose them to her daughter.

"How is the career searching going?" asked Donna, redirecting the conversation.

"Well, I've been giving some more thought to your art teacher suggestion. And I think that I can see myself doing that. But I started researching the requirements, and found out that if I get a certification in one state, I can't get a job with it in another state."

"What are you saying Silvia? So now you want to move again? Why? Where?" Donna was being really rambunctious and edgy on this particular evening and Silvia, hearing the frustration in her mother's voice, was reluctant to continue talking. Fortunately, Donna then took on a much more empathetic tone of voice, and she apologized.

"I'm sorry honey. I had a long day. I didn't mean to snap. I just wish that you could stop moving. I think it's going to be hard for you to ever create any kind of nice life for yourself if you're always moving. And what would be so terrible about getting a certification here and staying in New Jersey? It's not such a terrible place. You do have your family here."

She could never tell her mother that she felt that she could never start over here, that it felt stale, that she felt trapped here and that the thought of staying frightened her. Silvia just told her that she would think about it, and she was very happy when her mother changed the subject once again.

"How's Vince?" asked Donna.

"He's doing alright, except he's still worried about whether or not Dad will help him with his tuition."

"Oh, I know he will when it's all said and done."

"I'm going to tell him about the party tonight when I get home. Oh, and I think Dad's going to go for it, after all."

"That's great," said Donna, the tone in her voice not conveying that she genuinely thought that it was great.

"I don't know. For some reason, you don't sound too happy about it Mom." There was an uncomfortable silence, which was rare in a conversation with Donna.

"It's not that. I *am* happy about it. And I'm so grateful to you honey. It's just that I think it would be best if I wasn't there."

Although Silvia was taken aback by her mother's sudden shift, she had no time to fret or to figure it out. Her need to make the reunion happen was stronger than ever, and she needed to say something in an effort to undo Donna's change of heart and convince her that she needed to be there. Being well-aware of Donna's weakness for Vince, she knew just what to say: "Mom, how would Vince feel if you weren't there?"

"I was thinking that he and I could celebrate on our own. I'll take him to some nice restaurant."

"It won't be the same, Mom."

"Let me think about it, honey."

Silvia could tell that her mother had much more to divulge, and assumed that if she was a friend and not her daughter, she would tell her that she was finally making a successful break from Frank, and that seeing him might stir up feelings that she couldn't risk experiencing at this crucial time. So, Silvia gave it a break with every intention to return to convincing Donna to attend the reunion at a later time.

Donna then told her the main reason for her call. Today was the fifteenth year anniversary of her mother's death, and this year, for some reason, she was really feeling it, and really needed to talk to Silvia, who she knew was more bonded to her mother than she, herself, was. Silvia remembered and commemorated this occasion in some way every year, but this year, with all that was on her plate, the date slipped her mind. She now supposed it was more than just coincidental that she went to the beach today, as this was the place where she most strongly felt her grandma's presence.

Silvia's other siblings didn't understand her need to commemorate this occasion, as they didn't have the closeness with their grandma that she had. Grandma Tucci wasn't the type of person to show favoritism outwardly, but Silvia was her favorite of all the grandchildren. And that was a tough contest to win, as she had, altogether, fifteen grandchildren. Donna also knew and accepted that her mother was closer to her daughter than she herself was, just as she had accepted the fact that she lacked the maternal instinct that her own mother had mastered. It was Grandma Tucci who sat beside Silvia when she was sick in bed, who made her tortellini chicken soup, who shared boxes of Godiva chocolates with her on the way back from their little shopping trips, who took Silvia for long walks on hot summer days, and cried with her when her cat died. It was Grandma Tucci who did the things that Donna couldn't do, maybe because she was too busy fighting Frank off.

But Grandma Tucci's husband was an even angrier and scarier version of Silvia's father, and it was surprising that her grandma was able to be so motherly to Silvia and that she had not been worn down and broken and weakened like Donna. But she was different than Donna in that regard. She seemed to have more tolerance and energy for drama.

She also kept herself and her problems sealed up inside of her. She never talked about her problems, and her crazy husband, who she could never leave because she was such a devout Catholic. Instead of dealing with her problems, she chain-smoked and went to church a lot.

Silvia wondered if there was a time when her grandma and grandpa, also known as Gilda (with a soft G) and Cosimo, were in love in the way that Donna and Frank had once been in love. They eloped because Cosimo's parents, who had come to the United States from the northern part of Italy, believed that Gilda's family, who had come from the southern part of Italy, were no good, or as they said, "morte di fame." Gilda looked stunning in their wedding photograph, with big dark eyes, thick lips, and a heart-shaped face framed in loose black curls. Cosimo looked like a 1940's movie star. In the photograph, he stared at his wife with adoring, loving eyes. But that wasn't the Grandpa Tucci Silvia knew.

As Gilda aged and grandchildren started rolling out, she devoted less energy to dealing with Cosimo, who had mellowed with age. She relished all of her grandchildren, but Silvia most of all. There was something special between them from the start of Silvia's life, almost as if Gilda had waited her whole life for this magical little girl to be born. Silvia wasn't sure why she favored her over all of the other grandchildren. She guessed that it had something to do with her sweet disposition as a child. She sat still and quiet when the other grandchildren ran wild and rowdily taunted each other. She and her Grandma built sand castles at the beach, while her siblings and cousins played Frisbee and splashed in the ocean. And she assisted her Grandma dutifully in the kitchen on Christmas morning, while the others showed off their shiny new toys to each other.

Silvia was most grateful for the special bond, and she cried so hard when her Grandma died that her eyes felt as if they might be permanently burnt. After a while, she began to feel herself crying on the inside as if her tears had no place else to go. She became emaciated from not eating and had dark circles under her eyes from not sleeping.

Then one night, she closed her eyes and saw her Grandma's face, shiny and glimmering like an angel looking down upon her and saying, "Be happy, Silvie." More than seeing this image, she keenly felt her grandmother's presence. After this vision, she knew that she wasn't alone in the world, that she would never be alone. She knew she would always have her Grandma beside her.

CHAPTER 5

REMEMBER THE BONSAI

Silvia had told her mother that she would talk to Vince about their graduation plans when she got home. However, she arrived to a fight between Vince and Frank. Upon approaching the back door, she saw Frank running around the house closing windows, which was something that he did when he didn't want the neighbors to hear him screaming. It was a signal, a warning, a precursor to the storm.

"I'm not helping you with your tuition either, you ingrate!" Silvia heard Frank yelling, as soon as she walked in the door.

"I don't want your help!" Vince yelled back.

"That's right!" Frank yelled back, like he didn't hear Vince's reply. "I work hard for my money!"

Frank must have sensed that Silvia was home because she was only half way through the back door when he ran into the kitchen to tell her his side of the story.

"See what that brother of yours got started this time? I don't hear a word out of him. He sits in his room like an introvert and when he does talk, it's only to be a pain in the ass." Clearly, he was trying to elicit her support.

"I don't want to get involved," she said, still somewhat tranquil from her day at the beach, her body not yet adjusted to the sharp and sudden change, like a sharp change in the weather to which she had no time to acclimate. She could have asked what Vince "got started," but she was sure that it was either imaginary, or that Frank had forgotten exactly what it was that Vince did to instigate a fight. It turned out that he had not forgotten, nor had he yielded to Silvia's wish for not getting involved.

"That brother of yours is giving me a lot of crap about some plastic bags I bought!" he said, with hope in his eyes that she might sway to his side. Although she knew that this sort of thing was typical Vince, she still didn't react to Frank. Her face remained solid and serene, while his face turned to one of a sad, lost beagle at his daughter's refusal to take his side. Silvia, seeing her father's disappointment and being well aware of his current state of regression to that of a vulnerable, needy child, decided to take advantage of the opportunity. She agreed to talk to Vince and would use the favor as bargaining ammunition when convincing him to pay for the reunion dinner.

When she knocked on Vince's door, he said in an annoyed voice to go away. She persisted by saying "C'mon Vince, just open the door." She could hear him get off his bed and come to the door. His face was long and tired with frustration coming through his eyes.

"I feel like a fucking idiot," he said, sitting down on his bed and burying his face in his hands.

"Why?" Silvia asked, confounded.

"Because I should never have believed him when he said he'd help. I should have seen that he was just trying to reel me in with his fraudulent offer. How many times has he done that to all of us? I should have known better. I should have applied to Rutgers too. It would be way cheaper than Berkeley, and then I would be less dependent on him. I don't want to depend on him for anything. I don't want to depend on anyone but myself."

He managed to say all this without any sort of break, making it impossible for Silvia to interject. When finally given the opportunity, she was at a loss for words. She knew that she had to get Vince to apologize to Frank because

Frank would never apologize to Vince. She knew that she couldn't delay any longer in telling her brother about the reunion. She knew that if she could appeal to his need for Frank's financial help, then maybe he would apologize and maybe he would be receptive to the idea of a family get-together for his graduation. And with her knowledge of what she needed to do, the words came to her.

"Hey Vince, you know he goes back and forth with all of us about helping out with money. I think he may have even threatened Angie in the past. I know he's been especially bad lately. But, maybe, if he wasn't so fucked up about Mom leaving him, he wouldn't be acting this way."

"That's not my problem," he said, shrugging his shoulders. "And who can blame Mom for leaving him anyway?"

"No one. But that's not the point. She was his only means of survival. He's lost without her. It's nobody's fault but his own that she left, but it still sucks for him. Instead of crying about it or trying to get healthy, he does the only things he knows how to do—drink and fight."

Vince looked at his sister like he might be able to understand and relate to what she was saying, and she took his reaction as a prompt to continue.

"It's always like walking on egg shells with him. You never know what's going to set him off. And he does try to provoke us. He looks for fights. But you can't give him what he wants. He wants a fight. It's a diversion from his pain."

"I try to walk away, and then he gets more upset. What the fuck am I supposed to do?"

"Just act really nice to him. And don't give him any shit about plastic bags! I know you like to be genuine around everyone, but I'm telling you that you can't be that way around everyone, especially around people who are crazy like Dad. And the earlier you learn this lesson, the easier your life will be."

Vince's face was pointed down at the floor, and although he looked like he appreciated what she was saying, she knew that getting him to go along with her advice would not be easy. He was anything but a phony and couldn't help but speak his mind at all times. She needed something more to persuade him to go out and apologize to Frank, and suddenly she remembered something that Grandma Tucci had taught Silvia when she was angry with Donna. She told Silvia that a good way to stop being angry was to remember something kind her mother had done for her. The first thing that came to Silvia was the bonsai tree her mother had bought for her, knowing that she had recently grown infatuated with this type of plant and that she had wanted one very badly. She also helped Silvia, who was only ten at the time, to properly care for the high maintenance plant.

From that point on, whenever Silvia got mad at Donna, she would simply remember the bonsai tree. Even more than the tree itself, she remembered the kindness and thoughtfulness that prompted her mother to buy the plant. Now she needed to impart this lesson onto her younger brother.

"Hey Vince, I know that Dad has a lot of bad qualities and that he can be a real jerk, but sometimes you need to see the good in him. You need to remember that he's not all bad. You must know that we are lucky to have a Dad who gives us any help with our college tuition. You know most kids pay their own way. They take out loans and work full time while they're in school…"

"Well most kids don't have parents with money either," Vince interrupted.

"I can't believe that's coming out of your mouth. Since when are you so entitled, anyway?"

Vince looked down as if in shame and simply said, "You're right."

There was a period of silence during which Silvia hoped that something was sinking into her brother's head. She didn't want to break too long, for she feared that her words might then dissipate into the air. So she continued.

"Why are you always angry at him anyway?"

"Can you blame me? He's done nothing but pit us against each other for as long as I can remember. He's been terrible to Mom. He makes promises only to break them later. He..."

"Maybe that's all he knows how to do. Maybe he doesn't know how to be a better father or husband."

"Well then maybe he shouldn't have gotten married or had kids."

She didn't even reply to this last comment, as she didn't feel that it was deserving of a response. Instead, she recalled a nice deed that Frank had done for Vince and reminded her brother of this act of kindness.

"What about the time you had that really terrible flu, and Dad drove you to the hospital at like three in the morning? It was probably the only time you were sick in your life, so I know you remember it. I remember it too, because I came with you. And I remember him staying right by your bedside until you woke up in your hospital bed."

He looked like he might be shifting into forgiveness mode, but then his eyes turned angry again. There was something in Vince that would not let him let go of his anger. In fact, he had a tough time letting go of anything, most of all bad memories.

"Well, so he did a good thing that once. What about the time he hit Mom? How can I forget about that?"

"Do you ever think of all the times he came home with flowers for Mom? How he always told her she was beautiful? How sorry he was for hitting her?"

His eyes softened once again, and Silvia took advantage of the shift. "Be the bigger person and apologize to him, Vince. I know that he's much older than you, and that he's the parent, but you are much more mature than Dad could ever be." She knew that Vince would not be able to resist this last point. It won him over. He walked out of his room, begrudgingly yet compliant, and did exactly what his older sister told him to do.

When he came back, she gave him a big hug and told him about the dinner that she and Donna were planning for him.

"So I was waiting to tell you," she started, being sure to be ever so careful with her wording, "because I wanted it to be a surprise, but I was never much good at planning surprises, so here it goes. We're going to have a nice dinner out after your graduation ceremony. It won't be anything big. Just the family." She didn't use words like reunion or gathering.

Vince's face got really pale and his eyes filled with dread. "Please, don't, Silv. I don't want anything like that. When our family gets together, there's always a lot of tension. I'm under enough stress."

"Well, maybe Dad would be in a better mood if he thought that this would be an opportunity to get Mom back. And maybe if he was in a better mood, he would stop being so wishy-washy about helping you." She was as clear as she could be, but Vince still seemed confused by her theory.

"Why does a dinner for me have anything to do with Dad and Mom getting back together?"

"Because I plan on talking Dad into paying for the whole thing so that he can look good in Mom's eyes, and so then he'll think that he'll have a chance at getting her back."

As Silvia articulated this part of her plan for the first time, she was able to hear the absurdity in it, and although absurd, so was Frank, and so this sort of scheme had a very good chance of success. She hoped that Vince had not also noticed how crazy her scheming was, but she had no such luck. He looked back at her like she had a second head growing out of her neck.

"That sounds crazy. I appreciate that you're trying to help me out, but the whole thing just seems wrong to me. It's sneaky. It's not honest. And I don't like the way you're talking about Mom like she's some kind of prize."

He was right. It was sneaky and dishonest, but it was for everyone's own good, and she wasn't going to let Vince and his overly ethical nature get in her way. She thought that she should have been more careful in her wording, or that she might have taken the wrong approach with her brother. She had a temporary stumble in her brain, but then thought of something brilliant to say. "Well, maybe it's not honest. But think about it in the greater scheme of things. You get to go to Berkeley, and when you get out, you'll be ready to really do big things, to make big changes in the world. Dad might be upset when he realizes that Mom won't be getting back with him, but he'll move on. He always does. I'm sure he'll have someone else as soon as their separation is finalized."

It looked as though she was winning Vince over, and maybe she was, but he wasn't relenting that easily. "I'd much rather just the four of us go to dinner somewhere," he said. "Me, you, Mom and Cosmo."

"So you want to piss Dad off by excluding him, and you want to deprive Mom of an opportunity to see her only grandchild?" This negotiating thing was starting to feel very natural for her.

"No, I'm not saying that. Dad doesn't have to know about it. And Mom can always go up to visit Angie. Angie can always come down here. I thought this whole thing was supposed to be for me. So why should it be something that will make me uncomfortable? Something I don't want?"

She knew that he didn't like being the center of attention and that he would be much happier having a small, unassuming night with the family members with which he was comfortable. But this reunion wasn't something that was entirely for Vince. It was something that was for all of them, and his graduation was merely a convenient excuse for the occasion. Yet he had a big stake in this whole thing, and Silvia needed to say whatever she could to convince him of the importance of the gathering for him.

"Well sure, that would be nice and easy and comfortable. But what is more important to you? Having a comfortable evening out or having your dream of going to Berkeley come true?"

There was a brief silence, and she knew that with these final words, she had won, and Vince looked up at her with relenting eyes and said, "Well, alright then."

☙❧

Silvia was surprised to find herself waking up at seven in the morning so she could get to work early. Having always had a problem with punctuality in the past, she managed to get to work on time every day since she started her candy store job. Today she was even going in early. Maybe it was a new leaf, or maybe an increased sense of responsibility that was growing inside of her. She wanted to be a good example to the employees as a store manager, and she even took interest in boosting the sales. She never imagined that she would have cared if she received a shipment of blue whales instead of gummy bears, but she did. In fact, she cared so much that when she did get a box of blue whales instead of the gummy bears she had ordered, she called the distribution center and practically screamed at them for messing up, and demanded that they send a box of gummy bears to her store location immediately.

As she loaded a bin full with gourmet jellybeans, a mother and three children came in. These kids were especially cute and well behaved, and two of them were carrying child-sized instruments with them. The mom appeared to be particularly strict, letting them each have only five candies. One of the children required assistance in getting some candy, as she was too short to reach the bin that contained the lemon drops she wanted. Seeing this, Silvia ran over and helped her get out a small scoop of five candies. The little girl shyly said thank you to Silvia and walked over to stand by her mother. They were so amazingly well behaved that they seemed like they were from a few generations in the past.

Not all children were sweet and cute. They sometimes were rowdy, demanding, or whiny. Some threw tantrums with shrill shrieks. Candy was the last thing the rambunctious and hyper kids needed, and Silvia felt tempted to tell their mothers how their kids might be better off with carrot sticks and grapes. But she held her tongue. Besides, such advice would not be the best thing for business. When the not-so-sweet and happy kids came into the store, all Silvia could think of was how much happier they would probably be if art was a part of their lives. Of course, she couldn't possibly know that art wasn't already a part of their lives. She just assumed that they were leading art-free lives and wanted, very badly, to fill this void. She thought that the challenge of working with the more difficult children might be even more rewarding than working with the easy ones.

She couldn't wait to tell Donna about this latest realization. She imagined Donna smiling proudly at her and then asking if she had had a chance to check out any teacher certification programs. She imagined Donna trying to convince her to attend school somewhere in the area as she had previously expressed her concern about her daughter's inability to stay still.

Silvia knew in her heart that her mother was right. She might move to Portland, get another dead end job, and again put off getting into a meaningful career. She was starting to see the senselessness in her continual relocating and how much time, money, and energy had been wasted on all her moving. The starting over had been hard and stressful. She saw herself pushing a big box full of her stuff up a five-story walk up in Brooklyn. She remembered being so broke in Tucson that she lost weight from not having money to buy food. She saw herself being lonely, depressed, and freezing in Chicago. She remembered living in a slum apartment in a bad neighborhood in Philadelphia because it was all she could afford. It had been hard. And despite all of the many and varied experiences all of her moves had given her, they had really only held her back.

In part, she wanted to settle down simply because she was tired. Tired of moving from place to place like she was an outlaw; tired of sleeping on a futon mattress on the floor; tired of not having enough money to shop anywhere else but Goodwill and the Salvation Army; tired of being afraid to establish relationships because she would be leaving soon; tired of living in places with five or six other roommates. She wanted to sleep on a bed and not a futon on the floor. She wanted to shop for new clothes in real shops. She wanted to live in an apartment by herself or with one other roommate at the most. She wanted a cat, a boyfriend, and a place to call home.

❧

As she got off the old rusty elevator on to Cosmo's floor, Silvia smelled something baking and the aroma was intoxicating. Tired and hungry after a long workday, she was delighted when Cosmo came to the door with a plate full of fresh baked ricotta cookies. She wasn't surprised that he had baked such good cookies himself. Whatever Cosmo did, he did great. He said that the tree bark cookies she had brought over to his apartment inspired him. She bit into one of his cookies. They were even more delicious than they smelled.

"These are fucking amazing! Is there anything you can't do Cosmo?" she said, buttering him up for the favors she was about to ask of him. She had two things on her agenda: Getting him to go to the reunion and getting him to drive with her to Portland. She didn't really expect to achieve the latter at this time, but the former objective was definitely going to be accomplished tonight.

He smiled and stood tall releasing, for a second, the hunch that had become a part of his his body. He then walked into the kitchen to get the teakettle screaming on the stove.

"Tea?" he asked Silvia, getting out a box of Earl Grey.

"Yeah, thanks," she replied, sitting down at his kitchen table.

"How's everything at home?" he asked as he prepared their tea. "Dad still crazy?"

"The other night he and Vince were fighting. He said Vince was giving him a bunch of crap about buying some plastic bags. Dad's itching for a fight all the time, and here

Vince goes giving him shit about plastic bags. You know Vince though, with all the causes he's got going."

"Yeah," Cosmo said as if he understood completely. "I'm sure he considers plastic to be evil."

"Right," she said as though she didn't also oppose the use of plastic bags.

"Somehow I managed to reconcile them," said Silvia, with a look on her face like she could barely believe that she had accomplished such a feat. Then she thought of a way she could nicely transition into persuading Cosmo to go to the reunion.

"Every time Dad gets mad at Vince, which is like every day, he threatens to not help him out with his tuition, and Vince gets all panicky and depressed. So I explained to Vince that Dad is more edgy than ever because Mom isn't around and that he really wants to get Mom back, but he'll never admit that. I told Vince that having a party for him for his graduation would be an opportunity for Dad to try to get Mom back, or at least impress her with his fatherly generosity by paying for the whole thing."

She said all of this very quickly, hoping that Cosmo would not recognize that the plan was crazy. But of course he did.

"That's insane!" he blurted out, followed by, "And what makes you think that Mom wants to get back with Dad?

She seems happy for the first time in years. Why would she want to go back to him? And what makes you think that Dad's going to pay for a party? Unless we have it at McDonald's."

"I'm not sure that Mom wants to get back with Dad, or that it's the best thing for her, but Dad doesn't know that."

"So, you're going to lie to Dad?"

"No. I'm not lying," she said. "I'm just going to convince him that if he's going to get Mom back, giving Vince a party would be a great opportunity for him to do so."

Cosmo looked back at his sister disapprovingly and said, "What about Vince? He hates being the center of attention."

"Yeah, but I explained to him that if Dad has an opportunity to get Mom back, he might be in a better mood and stop threatening to not help with his tuition."

"Jeez, you really got it all planned out," he said with a tone of cynicism. "And what's your plan for me in all this? Where do I fit in?"

Silvia looked back at him as if she had no plans for him and innocently said, "No plan for you, but why wouldn't you want to be there knowing how comforting your presence would be to our little brother? Knowing how he looks up to you."

Cosmo looked back at her like he knew exactly what she was doing, and said, "So I show up because I'm the good older brother, huh?"

"Yes," she said, remembering that she could never lie to him or fool him in any way because he knew her too well.

He rolled his eyes, gave a small laugh and said, "And just where do you plan on having this party?"

"Well, first I should say that it's really not going to be a party. It will just be our family. I've just been calling it a party for convenience sake. Sometimes I call it a family dinner." Although she couldn't fool him, she also knew that she had to refrain from using the word reunion.

But Cosmo didn't seem too interested in her tangent on semantics and he simply repeated his question. "Where are we going to have this dinner?"

"I'm not sure. Some place near home. Some place..."

"Cheap," said Cosmo finishing her sentence.

"Yeah, some place cheap," she said as if to satisfy her brother. "Dad always mentions some place called Russo's. Says the owner couldn't make his whole legal fee years ago, so now Dad can eat there free whenever he wants. He's always offering to bring me there for lunch. I don't think they're very accommodating to vegetarians though."

"Russo's Bar and Grill?" said Cosmo, humor in his voice.

"Yeah, I think that's it."

"Yeah, they're sure not accommodating to vegetarians. It's a biker bar!" He was fully laughing now with his biggest, heartiest laugh. He then got slightly serious and said, "But it is good to know that the barter system is still in use."

"What about the Central Cafe?" said Silvia, not laughing at all. "We drove past it on our way back from an AA meeting. It looks pretty nice and unassuming. Not too pricey."

"AA meeting? You and Dad?" he nearly spit the tea out of his mouth from his urge to laugh. "Oh what the fuck. This is too funny. You got to spread this stuff out, Silv."

"What's so funny about getting Dad to go to an AA meeting? I happen to think it's pretty great."

"It is. It is. I'm sorry. It's just funny, is all. Picturing Dad sitting in one of those meetings where everybody introduces themselves as drunks. Hey, he didn't introduce himself like that, did he?" He then began to impersonate an imagined version of their father: "'Hello I'm Frank Greco and I'm an alcoholic.'"

"You know, you should take it easy on him," she said.

"Why should I do that?" he said, turning serious. "He's treated me like crap my whole life. And why are you defending him all of sudden, anyway?"

"I'm just trying to have compassion for people lately. That's all."

"Okay, Gandhi," he said smirking, "why you're giving all this compassion away to everyone, I wish that you'd fucking send some my way!"

"Why should I?"

"Because I spent my whole life being on the top of Dad's shit list for no apparent reason. That's why."

"So, you turned out okay," she said. And it was true. He turned out fine. But she also knew that he probably would have turned out a lot better had their father treated him differently. He probably would have finished school for one thing. Despite his brilliance and his ability to do anything and everything great, he lacked confidence.

"Yeah sure, I turned out fine. But I could have turned out a lot better if he hadn't called me a fail...."

Silvia stopped him before he could go any further. She knew what he was about to say, and she knew that what he was about to say was true, but she was also very aware of the damaging effects of blame. All that blame did, in her view, was to give the blaming person, in this case Cosmo, a way out of taking responsibility for his own problems, and therefore, a way out of making his life better.

"Cosmo Greco, I thought you were you're a bigger person than the type who sits around and blames other people for their problems."

"Well, I'm not," he said with complete indifference.

He wasn't at all the type of person who cared if she or anyone else thought that he was a big person or a small person. In general, he didn't care what people thought of him. He was born without a trace of self-consciousness.

"Well, maybe he hasn't had it so easy either." Silvia persisted, even though she was mostly sure that it was too late for Cosmo to forgive Frank.

"Well, that doesn't justify having kids just so you can try to fuck them up."

"I'm sure his intention in having kids wasn't so he could fuck them up, Cosmo! I'm sure that he was like lots of other parents who never bothered getting themselves together before they had kids," she said, and then continued with, "But what about forgiving him, anyway? Don't you get tired of carrying all that blame and anger around with you?" Truly, he, like many people, was carrying much more than he needed to carry, making himself and his life heavier than it needed to be.

Her brother still seemed completely unconvinced by her arguments in favor of forgiveness, and so she thought that now might be a good time to tell him about her bonsai tree lesson. She recalled Frank taking him for violin lessons every Saturday morning when he was a child.

"Do you remember when Dad used to bring you for violin lessons every Saturday morning?" Silvia asked.

Cosmo looked like he had forgotten about the lessons and was remembering them for first time in years, "I do," he said, without giving anything else away.

"Well, don't you think that was a kind thing? I mean, I know that you may have not been having the time of your life going to them, but the fact that he wanted you to learn an instrument is such a great thing."

"I suppose." He was indifferent, but indifference, at this point, was an improvement over anger and bitterness.

"I bet remembering him bringing you to those lessons makes you feel a lot better, as opposed to remembering the times that he put you down." She was careful not to say the word failure to him.

Cosmo had a look that Silvia never saw before, as if he might have been convinced, or, at least, mildly convinced. While he said nothing, seeing the expression on his face was satisfying enough for Silvia.

"More tea?" he asked, getting up to refill the kettle.

"Sure," she said. She suspected that he was trying to divert the course of the conversation in order to avoid telling her that maybe she had a valid point about Frank. She also knew that he was attempting to get out of giving her a definite response about coming to the reunion. He should know better. He should know that she wasn't the type of person to relent so easily.

"So, you're going to come to the dinner?" She said this more like a statement than a question.

"Oh, so now you're calling it a dinner?" he said, still unwilling to give her a definite response. She said nothing to his pointless question. Instead, she just sat there, expressionless, waiting for an answer.

"Alright, I'll be there," he said, reluctance in his voice.

"Thank you. It will mean a lot to Vince."

"Yeah, right," he said begrudgingly.

Silvia took a brief moment without talking to eat a third cookie and just savor its deliciousness. Then she was on to the next item on her agenda.

"So, have you given any more thought to coming to Portland?"

"Jesus Christ! What did you come over here for anyway? To ask for favors?"

"That, and to eat cookies," she said smiling.

Cosmo slanted his lips and shook his head back and forth as if this was the very sort of behavior that he had grown to expect from his sister. "No, I haven't given it any more thought. But it seems like a crazy thing to do. To leave my secure, decent paying job and move to a place where I'd probably be lucky to get a job as a barista in some trendy café."

He was right, and she knew it, but she persisted none-the-less, "Why don't you just drive out there with me, and see how you like it there?"

"I'll think about it."

"I'll pay for your plane ticket back."

"Well, that's very nice. But, I still need to think about it."

"It could just be like a little vacation for you. Don't you want to get away?"

"Not really."

She couldn't understand his way of life. She couldn't imagine him not wanting to move out of Philadelphia, let alone not take a vacation. How could he not be bored out of his mind?

"Maybe you don't think you want to get away, but once you do, you'll realize how much you wanted it all along."

He just looked back at her as if to say that there was nothing but nonsense coming out of her mouth. And although she knew that she sounded kind of ridiculous, she believed in her words. She believed that she spoke the truth. She also knew that convincing Cosmo of this *truth* was just not happening. Not tonight anyway.

CHAPTER 6
LIGHTNING BUGS
AT DUSK

As soon as Silvia got back to Frank's house, she went to her room to find her lonely self-portrait screaming out for company. She had neglected the painting for just the right amount of time, and now she could return to it with fresh eyes. Often times, she would not know what she wanted to paint and would start painting and let the image come to her. Now, she found herself painting her mother's face and so she decided that this work of art was destined to be a family portrait.

She wanted to capture the sparkle that had been in Donna's face before Frank wore her down– the sparkle that was just starting to reemerge. Silvia wanted to show the love that her mom had had for her children coming through her eyes. She wanted to get the way her skin shone even when she was tired and the way she always looked so held together and sure of herself, even when she wasn't. She painted her mother on the edge of the canvas, leaving room between herself and Donna for other family members. The two of them needed some space between them.

Vince would be right beside Donna, as they needed no space. She wanted to paint the way that his eyes shone with earnestness and honesty; the way his bleeding heart bled through his skin; the way he was always going forward, as if backwards wasn't even an option; the way he looked, acted, and moved through life, like a superhero of sorts. Maybe Thor, or even Superman.

When she was finished with Vince, she started on Cosmo, who she placed on the right side of herself, as he was without a doubt, the closest family member to her. She was so comfortable with him, in fact, that having him around sometimes felt like having no one around at all. He required very little energy from her. He didn't compete with her like Vince, or cast disapproval upon her like Angie. He didn't fight with her like Frank, or stay distant from her like Donna. He did challenge her at times, but a part of her must have appreciated these challenges at some level, or she would not keep going back for them.

She painted him looking kind of like a palm tree, tall and lanky with hair going in all directions. She wanted to paint his cold scientific rationality trying to squeeze through his goofy misfit self. She wanted to paint his eyes that hid nothing and that always seemed to know what was right. More than anything, she wanted to paint his hands, with his long, skinny fingers, with bulging veins. Hands so big that they could hold the sky.

There was just the right amount of room to the right of Cosmo for two more people. She absolutely didn't want to put him near Frank because she knew how bad Frank was for him. She knew that he would not want to be near Angie, but since she had only Angie or Frank left, she chose Angie. While they didn't like one another, they would just have to deal with being next to each other for this painting, and that was all that there was to it!

She painted Angie like the Snow White look-alike she was, groomed to perfection. But she also wanted to paint the sadness hidden behind her beauty. She wanted to paint the way she was always looking out, as if she had ordered happiness on a menu in some fine restaurant, and was waiting at a table for a waiter to bring it to her on a plate made of fine china.

She left enough space on the right of her sister for one more person, who undoubtedly would be Frank. As it was four in the morning, she couldn't possibly start Frank. The very early sunlight trickled in through her window making bright white spots scatter throughout the floor and walls of her room. She closed the curtains to make her room almost as dark as Cosmo's apartment, collapsed on her bed, and fell instantly asleep.

When Silvia came home later that night, she was relieved to find that Frank seemed to be in a descent mood, for tonight she had planned on getting him to commit to the reunion dinner. She went into the kitchen where he was busily cooking, sat down at the table, and tried to think of something to say in an effort to make conversation. She was treading new ground by attempting to make conversation with her father. She couldn't remember ever having a conversation with him. Her words always seemed to bounce off of him when she talked to him, and when he talked to her or anyone else, he spoke in monologues and left no space for interaction.

As she watched him move from one side to another side of the room, she realized for the first time in her life, just how closely he had resembled his mother. She used to shuffle around in the same restless, wasteful manner. Silvia usually thought of genetics as something that only influences a person's physical traits. She rarely thought of it as influencing something like the way a person moves through the world. She wondered if he had been this way as a boy, but she couldn't imagine a young boy scrambling about in this manner. She remembered she once heard about people becoming like their parents as they age. She then wondered if she would become more like Frank as she grew older. She hoped that she might become a hard worker or able to wake up early without an alarm clock like Frank. She didn't want to grow into a little old lady shuffling about in her kitchen. She visualized this for few seconds and shook herself out of the nightmarish fantasy by sitting up straight and forcing herself to ask Frank about what he was cooking.

"Sausage and peppers," he replied skeptically, probably because he was wondering why his daughter had a sudden interest his cooking. Silvia looked over to the side of the stove to see some stale looking rolls sitting in a plastic bag that looked as if it might have been re-used several times already.

"Where did you buy the rolls, Dad?"

He looked at her with squinted confused eyes and said, "Why do you care?"

"I'm just making conversation," she said, going over to look at the rolls like she was actually interested in them.

Frank looked back at her like he seemed to appreciate her attempt at conversing with him, as most people stayed away, and he said, "I got them at Scaffidi's," with a slightly less suspicious tone in his voice.

"Oh, isn't that near the Central Cafe?"

"Yeah," said Frank, suspiciousness coming back into his voice.

"That's a really nice little place, huh?"

"I suppose."

"I was thinking we could have a nice dinner there after Vince's graduation." She was ever so vigilant about her wording and her manner of speaking.

"Oh jeez, are you still on that?" He took a second away from his cooking to wave his arm in the air.

"Yeah, I'm still on that." She was careful not to be defensive, even though she felt a strong urge to be.

"Well, you should stop wasting your time worrying about Vince. He's not worrying about you."

Silvia decided to ignore her father's attempt to cultivate bad feelings between her and Vince and persisted on with the one argument that was bound to compel Frank.

"It would mean a lot to Mom, you know."

"How do you know?" He turned completely away from his cooking and looked directly at his daughter.

"She suggested it to me." Silvia wanted him to know that it was Donna who suggested the party, but of course, she would never conceal the fact that, although her mother suggested it, she had recently become resistant to having any kind of occasion that involved her being in the same room as Frank. The look on his face turned from one of indifference to one of curiosity, and just as he was looking like he might be willing to reason with Silvia, the smell of burning meat came from the frying pan, and he was forced to turn his attention back to the sausages. He turned down the flame and diligently began turning the sausages over in the pan. Silvia was untouched by his sense of alarm of possibly burning his food and she waited patiently until he was finished doing what he was doing to continue.

"Like I was saying, Mom was the person who suggested it to me. She wanted to do something for Vince's graduation and thought that having all the family gather for a nice dinner would be a really great way to commemorate the occasion."

Another thought popped into her head, as she saw the look of interest coming through her father's eyes. Maybe he suspected that Donna wanted to get back together with him and that her suggesting a gathering, where the two of them would be present, was her way of trying to achieve this goal. As the egotist he was, Frank might believe that

Donna's desire for the gathering had nothing to do with doing something nice for her son, but that her intentions were to get reunited with the wonderful man she had so hastily and thoughtlessly left.

"I thought she never wanted to see me again," he said raising one of his eyebrows as though he was cracking a murder mystery. "Now all of a sudden she wants to see me?"

"Maybe she's having a change of heart," said Silvia, with all the deception and manipulation she could muster up in one sentence.

"Yeah, maybe she is," he said in a self-congratulatory tone of voice. He put some sausages and peppers into a roll and grabbed a can of beer from the refrigerator.

Silvia let her father take a moment to enjoy his imagined achievement before getting back to her cause. "Well, I was thinking that the Central Cafe would be perfect for the occasion, Dad," she said with a hopeful smile. "What do you think?" She knew how much he loved it when anyone, especially his children, requested his advice or opinion, as they did so very infrequently.

"I suppose," he said, shoving some of a sandwich in his mouth. As he opened his can of beer and took a sip equivalent to about half of the can, she thought of saying something to stop him from drinking the beer. It would lead to another, followed by another, followed by another, and so on and so on, until he was throwing his guts up in the bathroom, passing out on the den floor or fighting with her and Vince. She wanted to say something to stop this cycle, but she couldn't risk annoying him, given her current agenda, so she kept her mouth shut. Still, he must have felt her disapproval because he walked into the den with his beer and sandwich, and in doing so, broke his own rule of eating outside of the kitchen.

She didn't intend to seem disapproving of him. In fact, she had grown less judgmental of him recently, replacing her judging feelings for those of sympathy. She had a dream last week of a baby boy crying out in the night for his mother, who, for some mysterious dream reason, couldn't be there for him. It didn't take her long after waking to figure out that the little boy was her father. Most of her dreams were forgotten by the time she got out of her bed, but this one stayed with her all day, with the image playing over and over in her mind. She wanted to feel angry with her Grandma Greco for being such a lousy mother to her father and most likely the primary impetus for his drinking, which in turn, made him be a lousy father. She wanted someone to blame. But then she thought of how she had just talked to Cosmo about how he should stop blaming Frank for his problems. She had to practice what she preached or she would be a hypocrite. Besides, maybe Frank's mother, like him, did the best she could.

Silvia walked into the room in which her father was sitting in front of the television, switching channels while he ate the rest of his dinner. The volume was turned up too high, as it always was when he watched TV, and Silvia felt challenged by having to talk over it, but she had no choice. She really needed to get a commitment for the reunion dinner from him tonight as Vince was graduating in a few days.

"So, should I make the reservations, then?" she asked.

"Huh?" he said like he was completely unaware of anything she had said during the past half hour.

"Should I make reservations at The Central Café for dinner for all of us for Saturday night?"

This time he pretended that he didn't hear her and just continued eating and switching channels. So then she used something that she had been saving for just such an occasion: The fact that his favorite child, Angie, would come to the gathering with Doug, who Frank had been uncomfortable around since he had made the drunk toast at their wedding. If he were able to make a nice presentation at the restaurant and get through the dinner without making a drunken fool out of himself, it would be a great opportunity for him to redeem himself in his son-in-laws eyes.

"I can call now to make the reservations for the seven of us and one baby," she said so tactfully.

"Seven?" he put the remote down, and looked at his daughter. "What do you mean seven plus a baby? Angie's coming?" He got a glimmer of light in his face.

"Yeah," Silvia said, feeling a great sense of accomplishment for getting his undivided attention. "She's really looking forward to it too." Frank didn't know Angie well enough to know that she couldn't possibly be looking forward to this event. He wasn't even aware of the conflict between Angie and Cosmo that had been going on since they were children. He would probably be happy to know of the existence of this conflict. He might even pat himself on the back for being partially responsible for them not liking each other. He had, after all, played a crucial part in the separation of his two children by making her his favorite and him the black sheep.

"She's coming with Doug?" He asked, as if he didn't already know the answer to this question.

"And Isabella," Silvia said, nodding her head.

Frank looked onto the floor for a few seconds and then at Silvia. She assumed that he was thinking that this dinner was a good idea after all, but there was still one thing nagging at him.

"You know who's going to have to pay for the whole thing? Don't you?" Frank didn't seem as angry as she thought he would be. She figured that the combination of seeing Donna and Angie with having an opportunity to look good in his son-in-law's eyes was more important than the price of dinner.

"Well yeah, Dad, but think of how good you will look in *everyone's* eyes." And when she said *everyone*, she was really only referring to Donna, Doug and Angie.

"That's true," he said, with an expression on his face like he was trying to visualize how *everyone* would be responding so graciously to his act of generosity. And suddenly a look of concern came into his eyes, and he said, "How will everyone be sure that I paid for the whole thing? I want some kind of public recognition." He said this like a little boy demanding a treat from his mother for his good behavior. But Silvia was prepared for this question.

"I'll say something in a toast I make for Vince. I'll give a special thanks to you for your generosity, so everyone will know."

Frank seemed satisfied with this agreement and told her to make the reservation. After she made her call, she was surprised to find herself going back into the den to sit in front of the television with Frank. She would normally retreat to her room and paint, write emails or plan her move to Portland. But she felt something inside that directed her back towards the den as if, maybe, for the first time in her life, she wanted her father's company.

"What now?" he said to her as if her re-entrance into the room was purely opportunistic.

"Nothing. I just thought I'd watch TV with you." When he realized that she didn't want anything from him, he asked her if there was anything special she wanted to watch. Her mind went blank. She rarely watched television and so she was unfamiliar with the current programming. She imagined that most every channel was showing some terrible reality show.

"Oh, whatever," she said. She was glad when he turned on a nature channel that was showing a documentary on giraffes. As long as she could remember, he liked watching nature and animal shows, and Silvia liked this particular aspect of her father.

He began looking around the room like he was uncomfortable and then blurted out, "I got the worst sweet tooth. Damn, I wish I'd stopped for some ice cream. They have Breyers on sale at the ACME. Wish I had some now."

Silvia knew that he was fishing for an offer for her to go get some ice cream, so she told him that she would go and pick some up. At that, Frank's face brightened and he made a special request for mint chocolate chip. "If they don't have that, get chocolate fudge. If they don't have that, just plain chocolate." She said okay, walked out of the room, and was almost out of the back door when she heard him say, "If they don't have any of those flavors, just call me."

"Righto," she said, and hurried out of the door.

❧

When she came back home, he was staring out of the kitchen window anxiously awaiting her arrival.

"I got mint chocolate chip," she said, as soon as she walked in the door. Frank looked like he wanted to jump up and down and clap his hands and shout hurray. He had the bowls and spoons out and he began digging the ice cream as soon as she put the carton down on the table.

They ate their ice cream while watching wild animals on TV, and during one of the commercials, Frank turned to his daughter and said, "You know something? You're good company." He said this as though it was a brand new realization for him, and in some way, maybe it was. She smiled as if to thank him for paying her the compliment.

"So, have you given any thought to what you want to do with your life?" he asked. She knew what he meant by this strange question. If he was more skilled at the art of conversation, he might say something like, "Have you explored any new career options recently?"

Silvia knowing full well what her father meant, responded, "I'm thinking of getting a certification in elementary education and becoming an art teacher."

Frank raised his eyebrows and said, "Now you're using your head," as if she wasn't using her head before. And then he added, "Too bad that teachers are getting laid off left and right these days."

"Yeah," she agreed, "but what isn't tough these days?" She felt like an old person saying "these days." He nodded in agreement, as he ate some of his ice cream.

"Where are you thinking of getting your certification?" he asked.

"I'm not sure," she said, not wanting to divulge her plans to move to Portland to him. She knew that he thought of her moving around from place to place to be completely senseless, and she didn't want to lessen the respect that he was now giving her.

"You can stay here if you want. It won't cost you anything. You can commute to Rowan. That's not far."

When she had considered this option previously, she felt sick in her stomach. But now as she sat eating ice cream, watching the nature channel with the mellow version of

Frank, she felt like maybe she could live here. Maybe it might not be all that bad.

Silvia had fallen asleep in front of the television set and was jerked out of her sleep-state by a particularly loud commercial. When she awoke, Frank was lying on the couch, snoring happily. She decided to let him continue sleeping on the couch instead of waking him up, knowing that he sleeps much better on the couch than in his bed. So she quietly slipped away and went off to her room. On her way, she stopped by Vince's room to find him talking on the phone to one of his friends. She needed to clear some things up with him before the reunion, and now was as good of a time as any, so she sat on the only chair in his room and waited for him to get off the phone.

As she waited, she stared at the walls of his room that were mostly bare, except for a vintage peace poster that hung crookedly near the door to his closet. She thought it ironic that he was so impassioned about the principle of peace, and yet, like all of the Grecos, he was unable to get along with the members of his own family. She felt that peace was something that began at home and if it couldn't be achieved in one's very own home, then trying to achieve it in the world would be extremely difficult, or even impossible. He needed to know this and he needed to know this now.

"Nice poster," she said looking at the peace poster.

"Thanks," he said like he was confused by her remark.

"I mean it's a nice symbol and all," she said trying to clarify her remark.

He had no response. He just looked back at her like he had no idea where she was going with her strange little comment, but his face became less confused when she said, "Peace begins at home, you know."

"Does it?" he said as if he didn't trust her words.

"Well, it has to start somewhere. It doesn't come from the air."

"I suppose not."

She was now beginning to get frustrated at his casual indifference, and so she began speaking in a loud, slightly angry tone of voice in order to get a rise out of him.

"How can you care so much about something like world peace if you're not at peace with your own family? If you want to make peace in the world, you have to start at home."

"I get along just fine with our family," he said defensively.

"What about Dad?"

"Who gets along with Dad?"

"What about how you can't stand Doug? What did he ever do to you?"

Vince raised his eyebrows, smiled sardonically, and answered his sister by saying, "What did he ever do to me? How about what he did to the whole country? The whole world! He's a criminal like all those Wall Street bastards!" He spoke loud and passionate like an Evangelical preacher.

"Oh, c'mon, Vince," she said.

"It's tough to forgive a bunch of criminals that are never blamed for their criminal activity. If anything, they're rewarded for it."

"Maybe he doesn't really know the criminality of the system he works for. Ever think of that? He does seem naïve, at times."

"He's highly educated. I think he's wise enough to know the difference between right and wrong."

"But can't you, at least, give him the benefit of the doubt? And if you were not so busy hating him, you might, one day, have an opportunity to get through to him. And that goes for all people like him. How are you going to work for world peace if you can't talk to people like Doug?" At this last statement, Silvia perceived a shift in Vince's facial expression that seemed to indicate a trace of understanding. Moreover, he didn't refute this last argument that his sister had made, and thus, she had an opportunity to expand on this idea. "You know that diplomats don't only talk to like-minded people. I bet most of the time they don't even like the people they have to interact with. But they know that they have to be diplomatic to accomplish their goals, and so they are."

Vince looked like he wanted to say something back, but it appeared as though he didn't have a good comeback to this one. So he just listened to the rest of what his suddenly didactic sister had to say about peace, love, and Wall Street.

"All I'm saying is that maybe if people like you could get through to people like Doug, we might not be in the state that we're in. Maybe if groups of people didn't hate each other and encapsulate themselves from each other the way they do, it might be a different world. A better world."

Vince put his head in his hands and looked down at the floor. Then he looked up at his sister like he wanted to say something, but could think of nothing to say. She could tell by the look in his eyes that she had gotten through to him, and that was good enough for her.

She said goodnight and went down the hallway to her room where she collapsed on her bed after what felt like a never-ending day. Her ears were ringing from her tiredness. She got up to change her clothes and then she did something with complete unawareness. She put her clothes inside the drawers of her old bureau. Maybe it was the fatigue that made her do such a thing. Maybe it was the nice night she had with Frank and the great talk she had with

Vince. Using the old bureau felt perfectly natural to her tonight. She even felt a small temptation to take all of the clothing out of the crates and put them inside of the drawers of her bureau, but she resisted. It still felt too soon.

೮෧

Silvia was glad that Donna decided to meet her at the mall for dinner. She was starting to learn all kinds of stuff about the mall. Probably more information than she ever wanted to know about the shopping center that she had devoutly avoided for most of her life. She was very glad she had discovered the restaurant at which she was meeting her mother as it had the best French onion soup she had ever had in her life. When she got to the restaurant, Donna was sitting at a table, dressed in a plain black top and glasses, reading from an e-book reader, sipping a glass of red wine. Silvia gave her mom a hug, sat down, and began buttering a piece of bread from a basket that was in the center of the table.

"How was work?" Donna asked, turning her reader off and putting it away in her bag. Silvia responded by rolling her eyes, which told her mother that work could have been better. So her mother, instead of persisting with more questions about work, asked her daughter if she had looked any further into the possibility of teaching.

"I did. I did. And I've given it more thought. A lot more. And I think I want to do it," she said, her face lighting up. "I would have to get a teacher certification, unless I opt to teach in a private school, but the pay in private schools tends to be much lower."

"A private school would be a great way to get in, though, and see if teaching is something you really like," said Donna, who then continued in a much more pessimistic tone with, "The only thing with teaching is that it seems like a tough field to get into these days. With all the lay-offs and such."

"Well, I'm aware of that, but what wouldn't be tough?" She was getting a little tired of hearing this same thing about lay-offs over and over again.

"True. True," said Donna, as the waiter appeared at their table. He tried to look awake and alert, but Silvia could see the exhaustion coming right through his skin, and she felt empathy for him. After her mother got through with asking him several questions about the menu, she really felt for him. Silvia thought that if her mother had ever waited tables, she might be more considerate to the wait staff. She also imagined that if Donna had been a waitress, she would have been a good one. She was quick witted and had both feet planted firmly on the ground, unlike herself.

She imagined the awful possibility of having to get another waitress job at some point in the future, and this prompted her to continue discussing her career plans with her mother in greater depth.

"So I've been considering whether to stay at home and go to school, or to move away to Portland and start school there. I keep going back and forth."

"Home?" said Donna, like she didn't hear anything but the word *home*. "I haven't heard you call your father's house 'home' in a while."

Silvia wasn't even aware that she had called her father's house home, but she took her mother's word for it. She also noted that Donna was now calling it "your father's house," and that Frank had been demoted, once more, in her eyes. Now she was referring to him as "your father" instead of "Dad" or even "your dad."

"I suppose I did call it home," Silvia said. "It has been feeling more like home lately."

Donna didn't seem to like hearing this and right away she said, "So, do you think you can live with your father?" She said this like she was prompting her daughter to answer the question with a negative response. This wasn't what Silvia was expecting or wanting to hear. She didn't want to be reminded of the harshness of the reality of living with Frank. And the most baffling thing about this comment was the fact that Donna was the person who had previously suggested that she live with Frank while attending school.

By the time Silvia's onion soup arrived, she was so confused and depressed that her appetite had dulled and she hoped that it would be re-ignited before her soup got cold. So she did the only thing that she knew how to do to get herself out of her current state of mind. She thought about moving to Portland, which was something that was sure to give her a lift. She even blurted out, "I'm just going to move to Portland then," knowing full well that her mother would react to this comment with disapproval.

"What do you mean? That's crazy," Donna said, putting down the forkful of food that was about to go into her mouth. "Like the only two options you have are living at home or moving to Portland."

Silvia was quick to notice that her mother was now calling "home" what she had just called "your father's house," and she felt satisfied for this small but worthy change of language. If her mother was going to play head games with her, she would play them right back.

"What are you suggesting? That I move back to Philadelphia for the fourth time, Mom?"

"What about getting an apartment near Rowan?"

"Why would I pay to live in this area, when I can live here for free? That makes no sense."

"Living with your father is not necessarily free."

"Well, he hasn't really been so bad lately."

Donna looked at Silvia as if to say that they both knew better, and Silvia, in turn, decided that defending Frank might not be the best way to go in this instance.

"You know what I mean, Mom. If I'm going to pay rent, I may as well just move to Portland and be some place I want to be."

Before her mother could say anything back, Silvia ate a big spoonful of soup and enjoyed it as much as she could before hearing her mother's response.

"Well, I think you should, at least, stick with a New Jersey college so you can get in-state tuition. I think you should just put Portland out of your mind."

"I can always get residency in Oregon and get in-state tuition there."

"So, you're going to put your life off for another year, while you search for a perfect place to live?" Donna said with frustration in her voice.

"Just because I'm not starting school right away doesn't mean that I'm putting my life off. I'm still living my life."

"I know you're living your life, but I also know that you don't want to spend much more time working at a job that...." Donna stopped herself abruptly and took a big sip of wine.

"That what?" Silvia asked.

"Well, you know that your candy store job is not the most rewarding kind of job for you. You know that you want to do something where you can use your artistic talents."

Silvia knew this only too well, but the idea of committing to a place frightened her, especially a place that held so many old, stale memories. She knew that her mother could never understand how she felt. How would her mother, who had contentedly lived in the South Jersey area for her entire life, ever understand? She could tell her about things like the caged lion she saw in Arizona, but Donna would still not get it and would probably think her daughter melodramatic to use such an analogy. She could tell her about how she realized that her restlessness was tied to growing up in such a disharmonious household, but then Donna might feel guilty for contributing to her daughter's inability to stay still. Silvia felt very far away from her mother even though she was sitting only a couple of feet away. Donna had no idea of what she felt, and stuck as she was in her cluelessness, she continued on, rather anxiously, with her plans for her daughter.

"I think you should try to start school right here in this area in the fall. Maybe we can get a two-bedroom apartment together. And, of course, I'll pay most of the rent. And..."

"Mom," interrupted Silva, "you work part time at a community college. How are you going to do that?" Donna looked down at her plate of food as if her feelings were hurt, and Silvia, seeing how she had hurt her mother's feelings, said, "I'm so sorry Mom. I didn't mean to say that. And I would love to live with you, and I think that your offer is so nice and generous. It's just that I don't want to add any more stress to your life, especially at a time like this."

"It is a stressful time for me, and speaking of being stressed out, seeing your father right now would greatly add to my stress," she said, completely changing the course of the conversation. Silvia knew that the conversation would be heading in the direction of the family gathering before dinner was over. Donna proceeded to explain to her daughter that she thought it might be nicer if they all celebrated separately with Vince, so as to give him more opportunity to bask in his achievements.

"But I know Vince, and he doesn't want to bask in anything," said Silvia. "He wants to get the whole thing over with and move on. That's why having one thing would be best for him."

"How about if just the four of us go out to dinner— me, you, Cosmo and Vince?"

"What about Dad and Angie?"

"Vince isn't close to Angie and he doesn't get along with your father. You know that."

Of course she knew that, and she also knew that Vince would be much more comfortable with a night out with just the four of them. But the reunion she was planning wasn't for Vince. It was for all of them. What started as a favor to her mother and a party for Vince's graduation, had evolved into an opportunity to bring peace to her family, to save them from becoming like her parents' families in which siblings sue and despise one another. Moreover, this reunion was for her own sake, her own happiness, and her own peace of mind. She was sure, more than ever, that if she could make peace within her family, she would have peace within herself. She would be clean and free. And she had worked too hard and too long on this endeavor, and she wasn't about to give up now because of what she could only assume was her mother's fear of seeing Frank.

"Why did you suggest having this party in the first place then?" said Silvia, wondering why she had not thought of asking her mother this question until now.

Donna looked down like a caught criminal and said, "When I first suggested having a party for Vince with all of our family, I didn't feel so nervous about seeing your father. In fact, when I first left home, I kind of missed him and felt really weird living without him. Like a part of me was gone.

But, then, once I got used to the peace and solitude and got used to not fighting and having to always be on guard, I realized that I'd rather be alone than with him."

"So, was your real reason for wanting to have something for Vince's graduation really just an excuse to see Dad?" Silvia surprised herself with this question.

Donna's face grew indignant, her lips tightening and her eyebrows furloughing. "No. I didn't say that. I just wasn't so uneasy about seeing him. That's all I'm saying. I also felt guilty about leaving before Vince was out of the house, but I must say that a lot of that guilt has assuaged since I started therapy. I now realize that what I did wasn't only right for me, but right for everyone involved." Her facial expression grew from one of indignation to one of pride.

"How's that?"

"Well, say Vince meets a young woman and falls in love and things start out good but eventually, she grows rotten. And say that because of my bad example, he stays with her rather than leaving. Then I'm to blame, indirectly, for him staying put in a bad relationship."

"What if he and this girl who's gone rotten got counseling together and worked things out? Wouldn't that be the best scenario of all?"

Donna wasn't stumbled by this last hypothetical and quickly came back with, "Some people, like your father, are beyond help, and in the example I was giving, this girl was one of those 'beyond help' types. I guess I should have made that more clear."

Silvia felt cheated. She was beginning to wonder if her mother's sole intent in suggesting the party was motivated by her wanting to reunite with Frank, rather than her wanting to do something nice for her son. Now that she had begun to feel secure in not needing him anymore, she had no desire to have any kind of family gathering. This seemed malicious and selfish, and these qualities looked ugly on anyone, but most of all on a mother. She felt a very sick feeling in her stomach, and it came on just in time for dessert. She felt she had been deceived all this time about the person who lived behind her mother's skin. She felt a big gaping hole between the two of them and could almost see the table between them falling into it.

But Donna must have seen the sadness in Silvia, who sat in front of her hot fudge sundae as if it was a plate of chicken livers, for she then proceeded to explain herself to her daughter.

"Silvie, I'm just starting to feel strong and independent for the first time since before I met your dad, and I'm afraid that if I see him now, I might weaken. It's a fragile time. You must know what I mean." Donna looked right into her daughter's eyes with a sincere expression that begged for some sort of understanding.

And Silvia could understand her mother's feelings better with this last statement. But she still felt cheated for losing her mother's support for the reunion. She sighed one of those big, loud sighs that older, exhausted adults are inclined to make, and said to Donna, "Well that's all good and fine Mom, but what about all the work and effort I put into this whole thing?"

Donna looked back at Silvia with surprise that hinged on shock, as if she didn't have the slightest idea of all of the effort that her daughter had put into planning the occasion. And she, of course, had no idea. Why would she? How could she?

"I had no idea you put so much into it. I guess I didn't realize it was so important to you," said Donna like she had some new-found admiration for Silvia.

"Well, it is."

"Why?"

How could Silvia answer this question? She couldn't exactly tell her mother that the reunion was so important to her because she believed that it could save them all from becoming like the families that she and Frank had come from. She couldn't tell her that she believed that making peace in their family might give her the peace that she needed to stay still and stop running through her life. But she could tell her that it was important to her because it would be very beneficial to Vince, and how could Donna possibly resist anything that would be for the benefit of her favorite?

"I happen to think that this would really be a great thing for Vince. I know he acts like he hates being the center of attention and doesn't like family gatherings, but when I told him about it, you should have seen the look on his face. I haven't seen him looking so happy since he was a little boy. He knows that I made the reservations, and if I was to go and tell him that it's off now because you don't want to go, how do you think that would make him feel, Mom?" Silvia was both pleased and disgusted with herself for being such a great, big liar, but she felt that she had no choice at this point.

Donna finally agreed that the dinner would be a good thing and said that she would definitely be there. Silvia thanked her mother and ate her half melted sundae with joy. But after her sundae ended, she returned to the laborious conversation. She thought about what her mother had said about not wanting to see Frank, and then she asked her mother the inevitable question: "Do you definitely plan to divorce Dad?" She looked right into her mother's eyes as she spoke, prompting the most honest reply she could get from her.

"Probably," said Donna. This seemed like a most lame response to Silvia, and Donna wasn't even looking directly into her daughter's eyes when she said it. On top of that, her appetite seemed just fine, as evidenced by her taking a bite of her chicken dinner that Silvia assumed had gone cold by this time. And as if things were not tense enough, the waiter had chosen this very uncomfortable moment to come over and check in on things.

As soon as the waiter left the table, Silvia said, "You know he misses you." She was confused as to why she was attempting to sway her mother to get back together with the person who gave her so much misery. But she wasn't trying to get them back together. She had already decided that this wasn't vital or necessary for their family to be at peace. She was just really upset by Donna's callous response and wanted something more from her.

"Well, of course he does. Why shouldn't he?" said Donna who apparently had gone through some miraculous transformation in the past month, for she was exuding confidence left and right, as if making up for all the time that she spent moping around like a nobody. She was her own person, separate from Frank. She was somebody now. Independent, confident, and vivacious, and she had begun creating a bright new life for herself.

"You're right Mom. Why shouldn't he? I mean you are a pretty, super lady." Silvia wasn't sure what exactly prompted her to say this, but she was happy that she did, as it made her mother smile bigger than she had ever seen her smile. There was nothing strained or broken or pitiful about this smile. It was full and effortless and happy.

༄

Silvia got home at dusk, when lightning bugs lingered in the yard and crickets sang loud into the air. She sat on the hood of her car and took in the beautiful night. At times like these, she thought that living in South Jersey might not be so bad after all. She thought of watching TV with Frank while eating bowls of ice cream. She thought of having dinners with Donna, going to movies with Cosmo, going to the beach with Angie, and seeing Vince when he came home from college. She thought of being able to see Isabella grow into girl and into a woman. She thought of having a teaching job and an apartment someplace right around here. It didn't look so bad at all to her. Of course, it might not be forever, but it could be for now.

The sky had a tint of pink, and the air was balmy and soft as she sat watching the magical lightning bugs appear and disappear. She listened to the soft breezes flow through the trees' leaf filled branches and the chirping of the summer time insects. She could hear Cosmo asking "What's wrong with here?" The answer she had for this question was now very clear. There was nothing wrong with here. Not one thing. It was absolute perfection.

CHAPTER 7

TOO LATE FOR SAVING

Some people are born with a smile on their face, while others are born with a frown. Silvia saw Frank as one of the latter and she wanted to be sure to get his sad frown in her painting, with lips bent downward like a horseshoe. She was determined to finish her painting tonight. She saved Frank, the most complicated person, for last. She would start him, like she started every person she painted, with the feature that she considered to be the heart of their essence, the thing that made them who they were. For Frank, it was in his eyes. They were very dark and when he was drunk and angry, they got blacker than black and hollowed out like tunnels that go nowhere. So that is how she painted them.

She had thought of making the eyes less hollow, less dark, and less raging, because she knew that behind his warrior facade, he was nothing more than a frightened child still crying for the mother who had never been there for him. But that very night, when he had slammed through the kitchen, his eyes had looked just the way she had painted them. So, Silvia was glad that she had chosen to reveal him as the angry bulldog that she knew he could be. Sometimes when he drank, it calmed his anger and allowed him to pass out into oblivion. Other times, the booze stirred up inside of him and made the fire within him burn bright, fast, and furious. Tonight was one of those fiery nights, and Silvia could practically hear his anger even before he began yelling.

He opened the kitchen door like he was trying to break it down and slammed it shut so hard that Silvia could hear birds, perched on the roof of the house, fly away in fright. He then proceeded to walk down the hallway, with heavy footsteps that sounded like his feet might go through the floor. Silvia could hear him banging on Vince's door, and opening it without giving Vince a chance to do so himself. She ran outside of her room, into the hallway, and could see her father standing in his fighting position.

"You're nothing but an introvert and an ingrate!" he yelled. "I never see you or hear a peep out of you until you want something!"

"Isn't that what you want? To never see me or hear from me?" Vince's tone of voice was low, calm, and indifferent, and this indifference seemed to infuriate Frank more. He then raised his voice and said, "Well that's it then, I'm not helping you with your tuition!" At this, Vince's indifference continued, as if Frank was talking about something incidental, like the cost of tomatoes.

Silvia went back into her room and hid her painting in the closet where Frank would not see it. As she was doing this, she heard his heavy, determined footsteps coming down the hallway towards her room. Her stomach filled with nausea, as if she had just drunk a glass of old milk. Her head felt disconnected from her body, as if it was floating above the rest of her. Her fingertips tingled, and she wished that she were able to jump out of her skin.

"That brother of yours has nothing to say to me except when he needs something! I'm tired of being made into a fool! And you want to have a party for him? He's a fucking ingrate! That's all he is!"

"Dad, calm down," she said, trying to have compassion in her voice. But this was the wrong thing to say, and although she knew that telling a mad man to calm down would probably not go over too well, she had not known what else to say.

"Get your stuff and get the fuck out of my house!" came right out of his mouth, automatic and fierce, like a bolt of thunder. Silvia's response was just as automatic. She got her backpack and grabbed Vince, who was all ready to go, and together they made their getaway.

The two of them were synchronized like a flock of birds flying south for the winter, as they got in her car and zoomed down the driveway. They moved in silence as they drove away, and Silvia remembered all of the times they made similar escapes with their mother and two other siblings. Usually they would have to evacuate in the middle of the night, when they were all sleeping, or trying to sleep. They would awaken to the sounds of Frank screaming, and glasses and plates crashing onto the floor. Angie would get up out of her bed and get her overnight bag out of the closet, and Silvia, being her little sister, would follow. There was no shock in either of them. No words. No need for instruction. Almost as if they had intuited exactly what needed to be done, like an instinctual or inborn response. They would meet up with the other three outside, and then all five of them would pile into Donna's car and flee the house. Donna would back out of the driveway, quickly and clumsily, with Frank chasing them down on foot, as if he, himself, was stronger and more powerful than the full sized car she drove. His limp seemed to vanish as he ran, almost as if the anger had somehow fixed him.

It was no wonder that Silvia was so good at running. She knew what it was like to always be ready, to never know when she might have to, once again, take flight. Perhaps because she had been trained in the battleground of uncertainty. This was why she could never be casual about moving. There was always some sense of urgency about her moves, like she was still running from her father.

She was sorry that she had moved any of her clothing into her old bureau but happy that she had not moved all of her clothes into the bureau and discarded her loyal orange crates. She was sorry that she had ever referred to that place as home and that she had temporarily stopped thinking of it for what it was and what it would always be– her father's house. She was sorry that she had ever considered living there with Frank or living anywhere near him, but she was glad that she had not taken any concrete steps towards settling there, like applying to schools in the area.

Neither Vince nor Silvia spoke until they were safely out of the driveway, when Vince asked Silvia where they were going. She told him that she wasn't sure, but that it would be "some place far away from that shit hole!"

It ended up, however, not being all that far away. They arrived at Cosmo's apartment where she knew that they could sleep peacefully, without being woken in the middle of the night by a raging lunatic. Going to Donna's would be a bad choice. It would just upset her. And besides, Silvia couldn't stand to make herself into a fool after she had tried to convince her mother that Frank was getting better.

Her head rattled with the remnants of Frank's tantrum, as she walked up the steps to Cosmo's apartment. The familiar dinginess of the hallway in his apartment building had become a comfort since she had been living with her father, and tonight, after escaping the madness of Frank's house, it was particularly comforting. She even began to see beauty in the vomit green colored carpeting and the peeling beige wall paint.

Cosmo came to the door, smart phone in-hand, playing some game that disabled him from saying a proper hello to them. Neither of them minded the lack of reception. They just walked in, sat down, sighed a bunch, and stared out into the space in front of them. Cosmo looked up from his game for a half of a second to say that he would be finished in a minute, but both of his guests seemed indifferent to having his attention and the pair just continued staring out into space as if they were asleep with their eyes open.

Silvia was sure that Cosmo knew why the two arrived together at this hour in a daze, but showed little concern. It wasn't that he didn't care, but Cosmo was the one, who stood with both of his feet planted firmly on the ground. Because he had his feet on the ground, he knew what was coming at all times. So it would be no surprise to him that Frank showed up drunk and kicked them out of the house. There was no distortion in his sight, and he functioned like a perfect mirror for the very idealistic Silvia, who was beginning to think more of her older brother's ability to live his life, and less of her own ability to live her life.

At this moment, she didn't see him as a quitter. She saw him as someone content with the life he had been given. He went to work, played his video games, went for the occasional drink with his friends, ate without analyzing every bite of food he put in his mouth, and stayed clear of lost causes and the arguments that such causes create. He knew simplicity. His mind seemed pretty Zen to her. It wasn't polluted with causes, beliefs, and ideas, like the rest of their minds. Unlike Angie, he didn't care what anyone thought of him. Unlike Donna, he would never get involved in some drama-laden relationship. He would never attempt to search for happiness in a bottle of scotch like Frank. He would never rant about causes like Vince. And unlike her, he didn't try to change people, go on endless searches for perfect places, or try to make peace in a family that knew nothing but war.

"Dad had another one of his episodes tonight, I assume," Cosmo said, putting his phone down.

"How did you guess?" said Vince sarcastically.

"Are you surprised?" said Cosmo.

"What do you think?" said Silvia.

"I think you thought you could change him," said Cosmo to Silvia.

"So, what if I did? Does that make me a bad person for wanting to help him?"

"No," Cosmo said, smiling deviously. "It does make you a fool, though."

"Fuck off, Cosmo," she said without the slightest bit of expression in her voice.

"People don't change, little sister," he said, flopping down in a chair without regard for her 'fuck off' remark. "Especially people like Dad."

He was right. She knew it, but she still couldn't resist telling her brother that their dad did, in fact, seem like he was changing. There was still the tiniest bit of idealism that flickered inside of her, like a candle struggling to stay lit in a drafty house. Cosmo turned to Vince, who then verified that their father didn't seem any different to him. Cosmo needed no further proof, and his face bore a smug look of satisfaction. So he was right. He was always right, damn it! But there was no time for being mad at her brother for always being right. There were too many bigger worries that had hijacked her brain and were now pressing in on it with the force and strength of a jackhammer.

Where was she going to live now that she had been kicked out of Frank's house? It was just like her father to wait until she was all situated to pull something like this. And what about the reunion that would save them all? She couldn't possibly think of quitting this cause now. Cosmo must have been reading her mind at this very moment, for he said, "So, I guess there won't be any dinner or anything for Vince's graduation, huh?" He sounded greatly relieved.

"No," said Silvia, looking up at the ceiling stubbornly. "It doesn't mean that, at all."

"Hey Silvia, I don't mind if..." started Vince.

"We're having a dinner, God damn it! And it's going to be great! Just fucking great!"

"Yeah, I'm sure it will be," said Cosmo as if he was trying to humor a mental patient.

"Do you still want to have it this Saturday?" asked Vince, like he was slightly afraid of his sister.

"Yeah. It's still going to be this Saturday at the fucking Central Cafe after your graduation! I made reservations! Angie is coming down with Doug and Isabella!" She shouted every word, as if she were making an announcement in a sports arena. She then looked back at Vince offensively as if she was expecting him to make some kind of negative response. She appeared to be very ready and willing to deal with him if he would. Vince, seeing this, looked down at the floor and refrained from speaking a word.

In an effort to block the noise in her head, Silvia grabbed the TV remote that was on a small, dented end table next to her chair, and turned on the television. She was hoping for something comedic, like a *Seinfeld* or *Simpson's* episode, but, instead, she got an update on the latest causalities in Afghanistan. This was even worse than the noise in her head. The war reminded her of her family, and her family reminded her of the war. Fucking war! Never ending fucking war! The thing that has always been and will always be. Arrows morphed into missiles. Sticks and stones turned into atomic bombs. No end and no beginning, just like the fighting that existed and would probably always exist within her family. She looked over at Vince, who looked like he wanted to jump into the television set and make everything right. She looked at Cosmo, who looked jaded, expressionless and complacent as a turtle. The person who knew how it all really was and knew that their family was just like the rest of the world. Too late for saving. A family of divisions and alliances. A family with so many lines that had grown thicker with time and would just continue to thicken as time went on. Lines that could never be erased.

"When will this war ever end?" said Vince.

"Whenever it does, you can rest assure that another one is right around the corner," said Cosmo.

"Yeah," said Silvia, her eyes transfixed on the television set.

"But why?" cried Vince. "Why does it have to be that way?"

"Because it is," said Silvia, who was suddenly talking like a realist.

"As long as people have been around, they've been fighting with each other," said Cosmo. "I mean, think of the cavemen. They fought with each other over buffalo and women."

"As long as I can remember, our family's been fighting too," said Silvia.

"Well that doesn't mean we all have to go on fighting for the rest of our lives," said Vince, surprising Silvia with his sudden concern for the well-being of their family.

"I tried Vince," said Silvia. "I tried to fix things in our family. Look where it got me."

"Where?" said Vince.

"Nowhere," said Silvia. "No. I'm worse than nowhere. I'm defeated."

"Trying to make peace in our family?" said Cosmo. "You'd have better luck in the Middle East."

"Well, I think it's great that you tried," said Vince to Silvia.

"I do too," said Cosmo. "Just a tad idealistic though."

"I wish I wasn't so idealistic sometimes," said Silvia.

"Why is that?" asked Cosmo.

"Because if I wasn't idealistic, I wouldn't search for things that didn't exist. I wouldn't try to fix people or to change things. My life would be a lot easier."

"You can't fight your nature," said Cosmo. "I mean, you are who you are. I am who I am. I wouldn't try to be a dreamer, and you shouldn't try to be a realist."

"That's right," said Vince. "And the world needs more people like you. Maybe you didn't make peace in our family, but at least you tried. If you weren't such an idealist, I'm sure you wouldn't have even tried."

Silvia could feel the look of disgust and anger melting from her face as Vince's words settled inside of her, and she lifted slightly from her bad mood to thank him. He was so right. Only a dreamer like herself would attempt to make peace in a family that had never known peace, and even though she was feeling like a bit of a failure at the moment, she could still recognize the fact that she did, in fact, make some worthy progress. She did get Frank to an AA meeting.

She did get through to Cosmo about how he should not blame other people for his problems. She taught Vince about the importance of peace starting at home. She taught them both about forgiveness. She got everyone to agree to go to the reunion. Truly, she had accomplished some important things. She wished that she could have enjoyed her feeling of accomplishment a little longer, but Cosmo brought her back to reality when he said, "So, I guess you won't be living with Dad much longer, huh?"

"No, I guess not," she said, her face filling with gloom once more.

"What about you, Vince?" said Cosmo, causing Silvia to turn away from Cosmo and towards Vince. Then a thought came to her. Maybe he would consider moving out to Portland with her. Together they could make a new, clean start away from the contaminated, stale, old part of their family. He could go back to school there and be completely comfortable amongst the other like-minded students, and she could have her younger brother by her side. In a matter of seconds, she had both her and Vince's life planned as the dynamic brother-sister duo living in Portland— the ones that got away, the ones that made it. And just as the sadness was beginning to float out of her body, Vince said that he would probably move up to New Brunswick and go to Rutgers in the spring semester. She felt a drop inside of her stomach, which hollowed and got cold and damp like a cave. When she saw Cosmo nodding his head in agreement with Vince's alternative plan, her head became light and distant from her body. She was alone once again. Completely alone. And it was probably this severe aloneness that caused her to make a spiteful remark to Vince.

"That'll be great, Vince. You'll be right near Angie and Doug." She knew it was the wrong thing to say, but she couldn't help herself.

"Why did you have to say that, Silvia?" said Cosmo. "You know he can't stand Doug. You're trying to start trouble."

She stopped herself from saying anything back because she knew Cosmo was right once again. Instead, she just looked away from both of them and towards the ceiling with an indignant face.

"What's wrong, Silvia? Why are you upset at me for going to Rutgers?" asked Vince.

"I'm not. I'm sorry," she said, turning towards him and attempting to wipe the disturbed expression from her face. "I just thought we could move to Portland together. That's all. Before what happened tonight, I was planning on living with that maniac. I guess I was fooling myself into thinking he was changing and wouldn't be so bad to live with."

"Why do you want to stay in this area, anyway?" asked Cosmo. "I thought you hated it here."

"You're right about that. But I was thinking of going back to school and getting certified to teach art, and I thought that if I went to school in New Jersey, I could get in- state tuition. I thought of staying at Dad's because it would be free."

"But would it really be free?" said Cosmo, repeating the same words that Donna had previously spoken to her. They were both right. The price of living with Frank was much more costly than rent would be in a penthouse apartment in New York City.

The feeling of being lost had taken her over once more. How she hated this feeling. She needed a plan she could depend on, a plan that kept her from falling down, and from having her world collapse on top of her. The feeling got bigger and bigger until it began to feel like an entity on to itself, a little ugly monster sitting next to her that looked somewhat like a grinning gargoyle. She needed to do or say something quickly to shake this feeling, or the monster would take her over.

"Cosmo, I really think you would love Portland. You need to get out of this fucking dump once and for all." It was true. His life here was no good, and she was now seeing the dreariness of his reality all over again.

He just looked back at her cynically and said, "How many times have we talked about this? Sure, I'll quit my job, so I can move with you to hipsterville. Maybe you enjoy poverty, but I don't."

She shrugged and said nothing. She wanted to say that she didn't enjoy being poor either. She wanted to say that she didn't enjoy taking dead end jobs so that she could earn enough money to move to the next place. She wanted to say that she didn't enjoy sleeping on a worn down futon on the floor, dressing in second hand clothes that she kept in orange crates, and eating pizza slices and bagels because that was all she could afford. She wanted to say all of this; instead, she said nothing.

She wished, in fact, that she could make a life for herself like Cosmo had made for himself. She wished that she had not inherited the Greco gene for being malcontented. They were all malcontents, except for Cosmo, which may have been the reason for her hanging around him so much. He was a sturdy, old tree in her life, and one that would not fall over or even bend with the strongest of winds. Maybe she was hoping that his contentedness could somehow rub off on her. But it had not. Instead, she remained stubbornly malcontented, like a typical Greco.

"Why do you want to move there anyway, Silvia?" asked Vince. "I mean, what can you do there that you can't do here?"

"It has nothing to do with *what I can do* in one place versus *what I can do* in another," she said like the answer should be apparent to him.

"Well, then, why do you want to move there?" said Vince, like he was really trying hard to understand his sister's rational for moving.

"It's because this place sucks," said Cosmo answering for Silvia. "In fact, the whole North East sucks as far as Silvia is concerned."

Silvia didn't bother defending herself out of lack of energy more than anything else. So Vince turned to her and asked, "Is this true?" She said it wasn't completely true. She said it wasn't all bad and that places like Burlington, Vermont might be all right if she was an old, retired hippie who didn't mind the cold weather. She said that she felt stale, tired, and depressed here. But she didn't say her feeling stale, tired, and depressed had anything to do with being Silvia. Nor did she say that if she lived in *any* place longer than a few months, she would get this same tired, old, stale feeling. She didn't say that she was apt to finding something wrong with wherever she lived and that, given the opportunity, she could find something wrong with any place. She did know, however, in the back of her head, that all this was completely true. She also knew that *place* wasn't the real issue at hand. Instead, it had always been her sadness that could make the most beautiful of tropical islands look ugly, the most exciting of all cosmopolitan centers seem boring, and the most inviting of small towns to be unfriendly. But what she knew in her mind and what she felt in her body had not yet come together. She hoped that one day they would.

ɞ

Vince slept on the floor, while Silvia slept on the couch. It was hard and creaky, and the gray blanket that Cosmo gave her, which looked like it might have been white at one time, was about as warm as a towel. Even if she had been sleeping on a luxury mattress with clean sheets and cozy blankets, she would still not have slept well. Her mind was too crammed full of stuff, like whether she should stay in the area and look for an apartment and start school, or move to Portland and put school off for another year or two and hope for the best in terms of finding a job there. Periodically, her mind would switch to plans for the reunion. As a result of the continual stream of thoughts racing about her head, she spent the night in one of those light sleeps, more awake than asleep, almost like she was watching herself sleeping. She could hear Vince sleeping soundly on the cold, hard floor beside her. She wished that she could feel happy for him for sleeping after their very stressful day, but in truth, she was jealous for his ability to sleep through the night while she lay awake with rambling thoughts racing about in her head.

She wanted to be angry with Frank for coming home like such a raging bull. She wanted to be angry with having to grow up in a house where things always went wrong, like all the Sunday dinners that ended in a fight between Frank and Cosmo, or like the summer road trip vacations with Frank turning the car around and driving back home just as they were nearing their destination. But as much as she wanted to be angry with him, she knew that he could only be who he was, and she really understood, now more than ever, that he could just not help himself.

She wanted to be angry with Donna for not leaving her father long ago and taking all of them with her. Why did she stay as long as she did and, in her own way, help to make him into who he was? But she knew that her mother, like most people, just did the best that she could do. And besides, Silvia knew that blame was a wasteful thing. That is what she told Cosmo and Vince. So why was she letting her mind go wayward now? The simplest and most truthful answer was that she was tired. So she got up and made herself a cup of chamomile tea with a bag she happened to have stashed in her backpack. Finding a clean cup in Cosmo's anarchic kitchen wasn't as difficult as she had expected, and shortly after making and drinking the tea, she nodded off.

༄

The sun poured into the room like it was angry with Silvia for sleeping in at a time like this. She noticed that, for once, Cosmo had left his curtains open and thought that he might have been trying to brighten the place up. This time, she wished he had not. The black she saw through her closed eyes turned into a reddish black, making her pull the blanket over her eyes, which did allow her to doze back off into a state of restless sleep. Unfortunately, she didn't sleep very long before she was awakened again, this time by the ring of Vince's phone. She could no longer fool herself that going back to sleep was even a remote possibility.

She could hear Vince talking on the phone to one of his friends, telling him about last night's events and refreshing the whole scene in her memory. She opened her eyes, and Cosmo popped in the room to tell her about the breakfast options.

"There's Cheerios or Cornflakes. Help yourself," said Cosmo, putting his jacket on and continuing with, "Gotta run. Just make sure to lock the door behind you."

"Hey Cosmo," Silvia said as he was about to run out the door.

"Yeah?" Cosmo asked.

"Thanks a lot for everything," she said, her eyes filled with gratitude.

She then moped into the kitchen to make coffee and eat a bowl of cereal, while planning her day. She would drop Vince off at school and go straight to work. She would probably go back to her father's house after work, unless he was still raging. She was planning to call him during her work break to find out. Just then, her own phone rang. It was Frank, remorseful, hung over, and apologetic. "I'm sorry, Silvia, about last night. I don't know what gets into me sometimes."

She felt like saying that she did know what gets into him sometimes and that something was alcohol. But she refrained. She knew that she needed to use the opportunity at hand to get his support for the family reunion and she knew that she would not accomplish this feat by letting him off the hook easy. She needed to use this rare occasion, in which Frank was feeling sorry, to make him feel more sorry than he felt already. And she knew just how to begin.

"Dad, Vince is really upset," she said.

"I know," Frank said. "I feel terrible. Maybe I had too much to drink last night." This was the great understatement of the year and not really worthy of a response, so she said nothing. Her lack of response was also a smart tactic. By leaving some space and silence in their conversation,

Frank's feelings of remorsefulness and guilt would continue to escalate unless he could say something to redeem himself.

"Just so you know, I'm going to be helping him out with his tuition. In fact, I plan on paying for the first semester in full. And the second, if I can."

But that wasn't enough for Silvia, who then said, "And the dinner after his graduation, Dad? What about that?"

"Yeah, I'll pay for that too. I already said I would." He had a hint of defensiveness in his voice, as if he might have momentarily forgotten his rampage last night. But still, his response was clear and there was no trace of reluctance in his voice. Silvia began to think that she could ask him for anything now, as he was so very anxious to buy his ticket to forgiveness for his latest stunt.

"Hey, do me a favor though," he said.

"What's that?"

"Don't mention anything about last night to Mom."

"I won't say anything to her, Dad. Promise."

ᏼ

When Silvia arrived at work, she was feeling grateful for being there and for anything that was a diversion from her life plans and her family drama. She was especially grateful for the box of yogurt peanut clusters that had arrived just in time for her mid-morning snack. She struggled with her tired, lazy mind to keep her thoughts clear and simple for the day, but her efforts were of little use. Her mind continued to race and ramble throughout the day and to fill with clutter and complication, all while she rang up orders, filled bins with candy, helped customers, and ordered the next candy shipment. She was at work in body only. Her head was filled with questions and all of the questions wanted immediate answers. When would Frank's mood turn bad again? Would it be before Vince's graduation? Or, worse, yet, during the family reunion? Would she be able to stay at his house until she could move to Portland? Or should she get an apartment with Donna in Philadelphia? Or maybe she should just rent a room somewhere in the area? Should she go back to school in New Jersey, or try to get her residency in Portland and go to school there?

She couldn't possibly answer all of these questions today. As Vince's graduation was tomorrow, she decided that the reunion demanded more of her attention presently than her life plans. Her original enthusiasm for the family gathering had drained out of her, like water drained from a bathtub once the stopper is pulled. She thought of all of the energy that had been required to persuade her family members to be a part of the reunion. There was Vince, who wasn't keen on family gatherings and much less keen on being the focus of such a gathering. And then, there was Donna, who originally suggested the whole thing and then, not only retired from the cause, but ended up against it. There was Angie and Cosmo, both hoping to avoid each other for the rest of their lives. And, last but not least of all, there was Frank, who was an energy drain just by being. Getting him to do anything, especially something that he didn't want to do, was a feat beyond the capabilities of just about any person. So her present state of fatigue was more than understandable. But with the dinner tomorrow, she knew that she would have to refuel her original passion for this whole thing. If only she had some idea of how she could do that.

❧

When she got home from work that night, the house was empty of people, but Frank's presence was there, everywhere, in every messy room, in every dusty corner, in every space and in every crevice. She could feel him shuffling around the kitchen, emptying bottles, pounding the floor with his heavy step and slamming doors. She could hear his anger, guilt, and sadness stirring around inside of him. She could feel her own sadness mixing with his, almost as if their combined sadness was creating a separate entity. She would never stop feeling sad for him now that she had realized that he had no chance for happiness. She had relinquished her cause of trying to save him and she knew that he would never attempt to save himself.

She went into her room, took the painting out of the closet, and stared at it. Last night, it felt complete, but tonight it felt incomplete. Something inside of each one of them wasn't coming through as much as it could. It was the something that was beyond their skin. It was the part of them that remained the same even as time moved through their bodies. The part of them that was who they were. She thought that if she could look at some old family photographs, she might be able to see what was missing in each of them and then she could paint the missing parts. She ran into the den, opened a cabinet full of old books, and pulled out a big box containing family pictures that had been thrown inside as if wanting to be forgotten.

She very slowly and carefully opened the box, almost as if its contents were under pressure. This box, that had been stowed conveniently away for years and that held their family memories, felt as if it was bursting with emotion– both good and bad. Pictures were thrown in like old playing cards, some curled, some bent, some discolored, some streaked and faded. A few really old, black and white photos looked like they had been taken in Italy, or *the old country*, as the people in the photo probably referred to it.

The first photo she examined was of all six of them at Stouffer's Restaurant in Philadelphia on one of the coldest days of the year. Silvia had worn her blue and white ski jacket and her new Levi jeans. Cosmo had just turned thirteen and, therefore, was too cool to be seen with his family. Silvia remembered him walking a long distance away from the rest of them for the entire day. Angie whined about how she wanted to shop, and didn't stop until they were finally all forced inside a Macy's for warmth. Donna worried about Vince getting frostbite. Silvia only wanted to look at the tops of all of the buildings. And Frank. Poor Frank. That was one of the many days when he blamed them all for driving him to drink. And to his great relief, Stouffer's had some pretty good happy hour specials.

There was a photo of their spring vacation in Florida when Silvia was five years old. They all stayed with Frank's friend, Joe, who he had met in law school. Joe had a big black mustache and talked with a slight lisp. He had a girlfriend, a dog, and no kids of his own, so he seemed to enjoy an opportunity to spend time with the Greco kids. He took Silvia out looking for seashells on the beach every morning. By the end of their stay, she had wished that she could trade in her own father for Joe, or as she came to know him, Uncle Joe. He went with the family to Disney World, where Angie got food poisoning on a hot dog, Cosmo got lost, and the Three Little Pigs sexually harassed Donna. No one could believe their eyes. The three, short, chubby, costumed men surrounded her, and began laughing like you would expect short chubby costumed men to laugh– like munchkins. Then one quickly put his pudgy little hand on one of Donna's breasts. Frank ran fast and furious towards Donna and chased the little men, but never caught up to them, as they hid themselves away in some staff-only area. He then divided the rest of the day between complaining about the event at the customer service department and contemplating bringing a suit against Disney World on sexual harassment charges. In the end, he decided that he would not bring a suit against them, as he always blamed such types of lawsuits for the cheapening and ruining the legal profession.

Then there was a photo of Frank, Donna and Cosmo taken right before Cosmo's confirmation. Donna looked proud, but tired, as she did in almost all of her pictures. Frank looked like he couldn't wait to get this obligatory thing over with. And Cosmo had the look of dread his eyes, as if he knew from experience what was to happen after the ceremony. Frank and Donna's father, Cosimo, got embroiled in their worst fight yet. And who could have foreseen that such a viscous battle would ensue over who got the last piece of eggplant Parmesan? Donna regretted not making another platter, but she thought one would be plenty. She had fretted for many years to come and had condemned herself as the culprit for this very unfortunate event. The occasion also marked Cosmo's last presence in church, and Donna blamed herself for this as well. She reasoned that, if the party following his confirmation had not been a catastrophe because of her failure to make more eggplant Parmesan, Cosmo would have remained a practicing Catholic. And despite Cosmo's various explanations to his mother that his transformation was a long time coming, and that it had nothing to do with the failed party, she couldn't exonerate herself.

There was a picture of Angie's wedding before Frank's drunken toast. The picture included Vince, who was eleven or twelve and looked really happy to be there. Who would have ever guessed that he would grow into an adult disliking his new brother-in-law as much as he did? Silvia was in a pink, long, puffy dress she was forced to wear as the Maid of Honor. And Angie looked simultaneously radiant and panicked. Her panic undoubtedly came from the fact that Frank might end up making a fool of himself and dragging her down with his foolishness. Her fears, of course, were well justified.

There was a photo of the summer of Silvia's eighth year when they had vacationed at the shore. They rented the top level of a house in Sea Isle City. It was a big, two-story square painted light pink with a dark pink canvas awning, under which Donna, Angie, and Silvia spent long, humid days sitting, reading, and listening to the ocean. Frank spent most of the vacation inside sleeping in front of the television set as he wasn't a fan of the sun. Vince built sand castles on the beach, while Cosmo sat beside him reading comic books underneath a green and yellow striped umbrella. At night, they walked on the boardwalk and went to the amusement park, which was Silvia's favorite part. She loved the rides that spun around, the cotton candy, and the freaky house of mirrors. She remembered it being a mostly mellow holiday, with only one relatively minor explosion from Frank that resulted from the high cost of a dinner one night.

"Jesus Christ," he complained to Donna on the car ride home from the restaurant. "I'd like to know when the hell food got so God damned expensive!"

"Oh, c'mon, Frank. We deserve one night out at a nice restaurant."

"Well, that's easy for you to say! You're not the one who pays the bills! You're not the one who's got to go around to all those one horse courtrooms like a fucking dog!" Silvia thought that, at one time, Donna may have tried to stop Frank from cursing in front of them, but she had no memory of her mother attempting this feat.

There was a photo of Donna's fortieth birthday party with everyone gathered around the dining room table with a big, white cake with blue roses in the center. Angie looked busy cutting the cake and serving slices to everyone. Cosmo's face had not yet turned cynical. Frank looked only slightly hammered. Vince looked too young to know anything about the significance of a woman turning forty. In fact, he probably had no concerns at all, except for getting the biggest rose on the cake. Silvia was smiling big and effortlessly like her family's gathering was all that she needed for her happiness. This photo gave her a shiver and even produced a tear. She felt a strong desire to get inside of the picture and to be a part of it.

She then came upon a picture of her riding her first bike at the age of four. Cosmo had taken the training wheels off of her little blue Schwinn and he and Angie ran alongside while holding onto her as she peddled. They let go of her when she was about half way up the driveway. She could still remember the feeling of exhilaration she had as she took her first peddles. It made her sad to remember that there was a time when Cosmo and Angie were at least close enough to make the joint effort of helping her learn to ride a bike.

The next picture was in the kitchen during one of their Sunday dinners, which seemed to last all day long. Donna was wearing a red and white apron, cooking busily and happily, and waving her arms about in a most animated way. This was before the day that Frank so wrongly pronounced himself a cook, and when Donna still reigned free in the kitchen to cook her delicious dinners that never faltered in any way. Cosmo and Angie were sitting side by side, as if they could stand each other, and even looked like they could pass for friends. Silvia was setting the table, and Vince was smiling big for the camera and sitting next to Frank, who had one of those tired, hard-working smiles on his face.

There was a picture of Cosmo and Frank playing pool in the basement. Frank was a really good pool player. Even great. Silvia was sure that he must have loved being better at something than Cosmo. This may have been the only photo with just the two of them together. Frank looked happy, or at least, mildly content. Cosmo had a goofy expression on his face, and jokingly had a pool stick pointed at his head.

The next photo was of one of their summer trips to Quebec. This was the Greco's traditional family vacation, which was something that began in Donna's family as an outgrowth of Grandma Tucci's desire to crawl up the steps of St. Anne de Beaupre Shrine on her knees in an effort to show her complete and steadfast devotion to her faith. Donna decided to continue the tradition with her own family, as she grew to love Quebec, and, in particular, Montreal. So they

237

all packed into their Cadillac in late August in the early morning hours and headed up to Canada. They stopped only for coffee and bathroom breaks and ate whatever they brought with them in the car, like chips, fruit, nuts, cheese, and juice boxes. Vince was at the center of the photo, a boy of three, wide eyed with curiosity, seeing the world outside of New Jersey for the first time in his life. Silvia was beside him, holding his hand in a protective sort of way. She took well to the role of looking out for little Vincie and she almost wished that she had been able to play the role of protector a bit longer. But Vince was fiercely independent at a young age, so much so that he often resented being helped. Angie was standing in front of them all, as if posing for a high fashion magazine. Cosmo was standing as far away from Frank as possible, undoubtedly due to having taken such a long ride up in the same car with him. Donna was looking straight out at the camera, her smile taking over her entire face. Frank didn't look angry. Instead, he was looking at Donna, as if he was still in love with her. The closer Silvia looked at the photo, the more she saw. His eyes were filled with both love and remorse, as if to say that he was sorry that he couldn't be a better husband, but that he was doing the best he could. If Silvia looked at any one of her family members, really looked at them, she might see this same sort of sadness in their eyes. If they could all put the sad parts of their eyes together, it would equal Frank's eyes. Almost as if the remorse that lived within Frank's body had fractionalized and was doled out evenly to each of his family members.

The next picture was of Frank and Donna on the Steel Pier in Atlantic City, with Donna's face glowing brilliantly and filled with love. The longer Silvia stared at this picture, the more clear Donna's ambiguity towards Frank became. Maybe her staying with him wasn't so much based on fear, confusion, and sacrifice. Maybe it was based on love and, as Grandma Tucci would say, "You can't help whom you fall in love with." She undoubtedly was referring to herself and to her daughter when she had said this, and, perhaps, to all the other people who had fallen in love with someone who was less than the right one. Silvia felt a great understanding for her mother at this moment and for her confusion, her sometimes selfishness, and other times selflessness. It all made sense to her now.

The next photo was one of the only Christmases she remembered that wasn't demolished by one of Frank's usual holiday outbursts. In the picture, Angie and Donna sat at the piano playing carols, while the other three decorated the tree. Silvia remembered Frank taking the picture. She was looking right at the camera, smiling as bold, bright, and shiny as a newly bloomed sunflower. It was the same smile that was on her face in the photo from Donna's fortieth birthday party and a smile she that had not had in years. When she tried now, it made her jaws feel strained and awkward. Only a person who was truly happy could make such a smile. And she was truly happy in this picture. She *was* perfectly able to be happy in her hometown in New Jersey. She had this photo to prove it. The words "you can be happy anywhere," spoken to her once by a friend, resounded in her head, and although these same words previously bounced off of her, they were now penetrating her skin, and going deep inside of her. She suddenly felt lightness in her body and a feeling of warmth in her stomach. She knew now that it didn't matter whether she stayed in New Jersey or moved to Portland because happiness really had nothing to do with anything outside of herself. It never did and it never would. She got one of those lumps in her throat that precedes tears.

But instead of crying, she got up and went in to her bedroom, with her energy for the reunion revived and stronger than ever. She got on her computer and sent out emails to all of her family members reminding them of the time of Vince's graduation party and location of the Central Cafe where the dinner would be held. She sent individual invites, as well as a group invitation. She attached maps to all the emails, even though she knew they all knew just where the restaurant was as it was in the center of their hometown.

She didn't leave room for RSVPs, thus not giving them an opportunity to say that they couldn't attend, to make excuses, or to be their usual cowardly selves. She simply said that she had made the reservation for a party of seven and one baby for seven on the evening of June seventh. 'What a lot of sevens!' she wrote, followed by 'See you all then', and closed with, 'Should be a great time!' She signed her name with the word 'love' which wasn't customary for her when sending emails, but which she knew was absolutely essential in this case.

CHAPTER 8
KEEPING THE GOOD

On the evening of Vince's graduation, the Central Cafe seemed darker than Silvia had remembered it to be. It looked as if the owners had, in these desperate times, decided to conserve energy by keeping the lights off. She thought that if that was the case then they should, at least, invest in some candles. She was glad that she had decided to wear something cheerful— a white and mint green dress. A few small windows allowed some of the setting sun to pour in, giving the room a slight glimmer. Just as Silvia was getting used to the darkness and thinking that the dim light would allow the family to feel less self-conscious, a brunette lady, dressed in red and yellow, turned the lights up. She greeted Silvia, who in turn told her about the reservations. The brunette, who appeared to be the hostess, went to check the reservations. This left Silvia alone, giving her an unwanted opportunity to get nervous about the coming evening.

There was still time to leave the whole scene, to weasel out. She could secretly use the opportunity to make her escape. Of course, she would never do anything like that, but she got some strange sense of comfort in the thought of it. This must have been what her mother felt like all the times that she had planned holiday dinners that had a good chance of being destroyed. Or what Angie must have felt like on the morning of her wedding, as if brides are not nervous enough without having to be apprehensive about what their father might do.

It seemed like Frank was always ruining or destroying something. He couldn't help himself. Silvia thought that he must have been the type of kid to stomp on another kid's sand castle. She recalled with sadness the time that she and Angie spent a long, hot summer day making blueberry buckle, only to have it thrown from the kitchen countertop while it was cooling, by none other than the inebriated Frank. Silvia, upon hearing the sound of crashing glass, knew just what it was. She ran in to look at her and Angie's work, splattered on the floor like the corpse of a person who had jumped out of a high-rise building. Being too young and stupid to know any better, she thought it might be salvageable. When she ran towards the fallen dish, her mother screamed at her to get away, gripping her arm as if she was pulling her up from a mountain ledge.

Would this night be a repeat of a typical holiday dinner, Angie's wedding, or the destroyed dish of blueberry buckle? Or would it be different? Why should it? How could she think that she was capable, somehow, of making it different than all of the previous family occasions? She stared at the red neon exit sign above the door like it was her salvation. She imagined herself escaping the place, followed by her family members arriving, dumbfounded, looking around, trying hard not to look at each other, growing in discomfort, wondering where Silvia had gone and wondering if something happened to her, something terrible like a car accident. She envisioned her mother calling the police. She got a strange kind of pleasure in knowing the extreme guilt that they would all feel when they assumed that Silvia, in her altruistic efforts to bring them all together, had been hurt or worse yet, killed. Maybe they would all gain some perspective, realize the triteness and silliness of their fighting, and realize what is really important in life. Their worry, guilt, and new-found perspective might even unite them. Then her imagination took a very sharp turn. She now saw her family members yelling and berating her, and seeing her as nothing more than a weak, little coward for running out on them.

This last fantasy made her jump up and zoom over to the hostess, with maniac enthusiasm, and check on their reservation. The hostess assured Silvia that their table would be ready any minute, but Silvia seemed dissatisfied with this assurance. She might have given her more specific details, like exactly how much of the table had been set. What about the cake that she had ordered? Had it arrived? Was it in the kitchen? She rushed back to ask the hostess about it. Silvia sensed that the hostess was treating her as if she was a crazy lady, but didn't mind it in the least. She was too focused on her present goal of making sure that the dinner was a huge success. Her little body awakened with new life, new nervousness, and new hopes as she began walking back and forth like her father would pace in the kitchen while cooking. And just as she noticed this, she looked up and saw him in the restaurant talking to the hostess and calling her by her first name, Anna. Frank spoke with all of the charm and charisma that he could turn on and off like a light switch, making her laugh and even blush. His eyes met with his daughter's eyes that returned his look with a combination of approval and admiration. In his return gaze, Frank's face said, "I came through. I did what was right. I'm here." And he was here! In fact, he was the first one to show up. He was even well-dressed in a gray suit and a light blue button-down shirt.

There was still a possibility that one or more of the others would not show up, but Frank was here and, therefore, she had succeeded! She felt a relief in her stomach that spread throughout the rest of her body, all the way into her toes and fingertips. The rest would be cake, which Anna had then confirmed was sitting on a counter top in the kitchen.

"It's carrot cake, right?" asked Silvia, still some nervousness in her voice.

"I think so," said Anna, who was beginning to seem almost as nervous as Silvia, like Silvia's anxiety had somehow spread.

"We had better make sure," said Silvia, biting on one of her nails.

"I'm sure it's carrot, and it will be great," said Frank, who all of sudden seemed to be taking on the role of the calm, together one. It was a role that he rarely was able to play and he seemed to enjoy this role. Silvia knew that in his heart of hearts, he would rather build than destroy. Destroying had just become a habit, and habits are, after all, hard to break.

She felt a sort of calm from his reassurance and for a couple of minutes she remained stationary and made a conscious effort to not pace or check on cakes and tables. Just as she began sinking into a state of calm, Donna walked in. Again, Silvia's body filled with tension. This was the first time that her mother and Frank had seen each other since she had left him. Why couldn't Angie have shown up first? Angie would have had little Isabella with her who would be running around and distracting everyone with her cuteness. Silvia now wished she had sent individual emails with different times for everyone, so as to prevent the very awkward moment.

Donna saw Frank, and Frank saw Donna, and Silvia saw both pairs of their eyes meet. Their eyes reflected a wide array of feelings: Discomfort, resentment, sadness, love, anger, remorse and lost hope. Donna did what she could to kill the awkwardness by saying "Hello Frank," as if there was nothing wrong. As if she had never left. As if he had never hurt her time and again. As if the big space between them didn't exist. He didn't say anything, but not because he was ignoring her. It was almost as if he had forgotten how to talk. He sat there with his mouth open, gazing at his wife, who looked absolutely lovely. Silvia wondered how her mother's radiance made Frank feel. Whenever Silvia saw an ex-boyfriend, she hoped he would look bad. This would give her a sense of satisfaction, as if her leaving him was the cause of his deterioration and ruination. If she ever saw one looking as good as her mother looked right now, she would be miserable. And misery was exactly what she saw in her father's face. Surely, he was regretting how much he had messed things up. He must be kicking himself so hard right now. But through the self-berating, the regretting and the misery, he finally did manage to say a hello. It was a somber, painstaking hello, without the mention of her name, but still, it was a hello.

Silvia decided rather abruptly that she couldn't take another second of this tension and got up to greet her mother. As she stood up, she saw Anna, who also just witnessed the exchange. Silvia decided that this innocent bystander would be a perfect distraction from the moment's awkwardness. She approached Anna as if she was her long lost friend and introduced her to Donna. She then turned to Donna and said, "Anna has everything under control, so there's no need for any worry." Donna didn't look in the slightest bit worried and her daughter's comment brought on a look of confusion upon her face. Silvia's comment may not have been the only thing making Donna confused. She may have been wondering why her daughter was being so charming? Like she had suddenly inherited her father's charm. Silvia had no regard for her mother's confusion, as she was only concerned with dispersing some of the tension. Anna's presence did serve to assuage the tension, and soon they were all involved in a conversation about her.

It turned out that she had just begun work at the restaurant a month ago, and that she was going to school full time. She was doing coursework to get her teacher certification and this fact spurred another conversation between Silvia and herself. Even more of the tension dissipated, as both Frank and Donna joined in the dialog between their daughter and Anna.

"Well, I think teaching is a great idea," said Frank to Silvia. "Now you're using your head." He would probably continue to re-use this "using your head" phrase with Silvia, but she didn't mind it. She did, however, notice her mother's eyes rolling slightly back in her head at Frank's remark, so she did what she could to detract from any more attention paid to her father's comment by saying, "I have Mom to thank for the suggestion." Frank looked at Donna, his eyes still sad.

"Anna," yelled a stout man with a round face from the hostess stand. Anna excused herself, and left the three of them to wonder what to talk about next.

"The ceremony was nice," said Donna, breaking the silence that seemed long.

"Yeah, it was nice. Short and sweet," said Silvia, smiling a nervous smile.

Frank looked down guiltily, which led Silvia to assume that he missed the graduation ceremony. It would have been surprising if he had gone considering that he had not gone to any of their graduation ceremonies, except for Angie's. And just when this assumption was cemented in Silvia's mind, Frank raised his head up and said, "Yes, it was nice," leaving both his daughter and wife with surprised expressions on their faces.

"You went? That's great!" Silvia talked to her father as if she was commending a first grade student for answering a question correctly. She wondered if her father's attendance had something to do with his guilt over lashing out at her and Vince earlier that week. She then noticed her mother look at him with a new found reverence.

Silvia looked back at her father and noticed just how tired he looked. His worry lines were so thick that they looked as if they were drawn on his face with a black felt marker. His eyelids looked so heavy, as if they were being pushed down over his eyes against their own will. Maybe he *was* tired. Tired of fighting over nothing, tired of drinking, tired of passing out, and tired of being tired. Maybe he was at a crossroad. He wasn't too old. He still could change.

And just as Silvia began to float into her fantasy world where miraculous transformations of character occur, where there is no fighting, where everyone gets along all the time and lives in harmony, Cosmo appeared in the doorway of the restaurant. People seemed to be showing up in the reverse order that she would have preferred. When Frank excused himself to get a drink at the bar, Silvia not only understood his actions, but also had wished that she too could excuse herself and join him in a drink. The idea of drinking with her father always repulsed her, as he seemed to delight in her having a drink, and this seemed very wrong to her. But, right now, she didn't care about his bad parenting skills. She cared more about releasing the tension in her body, for it was almost too much for her little self to contain.

"Hey," said Cosmo, entering the room as his usual self, dressed in mismatched clothing and a fedora hat, undoubtedly to hide his wild hair.

"Hi Cosmo," said Frank on his way to the bar, like he had just seen his son yesterday.

"Hey Dad," Cosmo said, with much of the same indifference as his father. Then he walked over to where his mother and sister were standing and gave them both a hug.

"Thanks for coming Cosmo," said Silvia, giving him a hug.

"Sure," he said. And then he just stood there and calmly stared out into the space in front of him. His mellow presence should have calmed Silvia. Instead, it made her more anxious, as if she was compensating for his lack of nervousness by being more nervous herself.

"So how are things, Cosmo? I haven't heard from you in so long," said Donna, hinting that she felt hurt by his apparent lack of correspondence.

"Oh, I'm sorry I didn't call you back last week, Mom. I've been crazy busy with work and..." He stopped talking suddenly when he looked as his mother's face, like he had realized in that second how awful it must have felt to be given that 'busy' excuse by your own son. It was so rare to see any bit of guilt in Cosmo's face, but Silvia was seeing it now.

"Oh don't worry about it," said Donna, who must have been sensing her son's remorse.

"Thanks for understanding Mom," said Cosmo.

"I was thinking we could go for lunch or dinner sometime soon," said Donna to Cosmo.

Cosmo agreed and smiled like he was grateful for his mother's forgiveness and for her friendship. Silvia figured that Cosmo had been avoiding getting enmeshed in any drama between Donna and Frank. He avoided drama like a gangster avoided the law.

And as the three of them experienced a mutual moment of togetherness and calm, Frank re-entered the room, drink in hand, and once again tension filled the air—loud, thick, and heavy. Silvia had to say something frivolous about something like the weather, or better yet, cake.

"We got a great looking carrot cake in the back. That's Vince's favorite. I think it's a lot of people's favorite. I prefer it to chocolate cake myself." She knew how little they must have genuinely cared about her feelings for carrot cake but they all pretended that what she was saying was something very interesting.

"Yeah, I love carrot cake myself," said Frank, who loved all sweets. Donna and Cosmo nodded, grinning in agreement, and just as their exchange about carrot cake grew into a thing of great beauty, Angie came in the door with Doug and little Isabella dressed in a pink, plaid jumper and looking all ready for a party. Frank's face brightened with smiling lips and cheerfully squinting eyes. Meanwhile, Cosmo's face became tense with worry lines and his body seemed to turn stiff. Silvia was surprised to see her brother react this way as he so rarely got anxious. He seemed to get more anxious as Angie came over to greet her family with her movie star smile. She wore black pants, an off-white blouse, and a red scarf.

Silvia smiled admiringly at her sister, knowing that it couldn't have had been easy to be with all of her family for the first time since her 'drunk toast' wedding, and knowing that she felt rejected by Cosmo and felt her usual distance from Donna. She seemed fine though. In fact, she was better than fine. She was happy to see her family and she hugged Cosmo as if all that had happened between them was forgotten. And with that hug, all of their resentment-filled past seemed to fade into the air that was beginning to fill with the delicious smells of gravy and garlic. Cosmo grinned, his shoulders came down, and his body seemed to visibly loosen as he reverted back to his usual caterpillar-like posture.

Then Donna embraced Angie like she had never done before, like she was trying to close up the distance between them. A distance that just happened and had been allowed to live and grow, unfettered and uninterrupted. A distance that was never intended. Could it be closing up forever, Silvia thought, as she watched the two embrace, or was it only for the moment? Everyone seemed to partake in the hug in a vicarious way.

Doug was busy chasing his daughter, as the five of them looked up to see the guest of honor walk through the door. Vince was dressed in his only suit, which was black and looked too hot for the season. His smile looked as if it had been painted on and spoke clearly that he would rather be somewhere else. It was a look of obligation combined with mild stage fright.

"Hey Vince," said Silvia, as naturally as she could, in hopes of relaxing him. He smiled his awkward smile at the lot of them. He walked over to Donna first and as they were hugging, Anna came out to say that the table was ready. All of them poured into the smaller private room that was reserved for large parties. The only table in the room was set with shiny white plates, silverware in perfect order, and maroon colored napkins folded like captain hats. The lighting was warm and made everyone look especially beautiful and helped Silvia to relax a bit.

No one wanted to be the first to sit down, as if doing so was rude, so Silvia broke the discomfort by sitting in the place where she sat at their dinner table at home, and by doing so, the others followed suit. She even moved the high chair so that Angie could be in her usual place. Doug would just have to fall where he could, which inconveniently happened to be right beside Vince. Frank was next to Cosmo, so that they could both irritate each other with their presence and their smacking jaws. Angie was next to Donna, so they could feel the distance that lived between them. Silvia and Vince were next to each other, so that they could compete over who used a smaller piece of paper towel as a napkin.

Why did her mother arrange it that way, anyway? Or maybe she didn't arrange it. Maybe they just masochistically arranged themselves to allow for optimum discomfort. Grandma Tucci would say that they were sitting just where they were supposed to sit. She firmly believed in a divine plan that permeated all aspects of people's lives, and she would have said that they sat in these particular places to learn something. She would have said that they needed to learn how to be more comfortable around people with whom they didn't feel comfortable. Vince and Silvia needed to learn to not be so competitive. Cosmo and Frank needed to learn to tolerate each other and learn better table manners. Angie and Donna needed to learn to connect with each other and to stop pushing each other away. Angie and Cosmo needed to overlook their differences and simply get along.

But Grandma Tucci wasn't here to say any of this. And had she been present, she would not have been heard. Her voice had always been clear, but lacking in the ferocity needed to be heard amidst the Greco crew. So, she went unheard to all, except Silvia, who was fortunate to know what was important at a young age. She remembered her grandma's words so clearly and as Vince sat down beside her, a feeling of non-competiveness came over her. She wondered if somehow the other members of her family were also hearing Grandma Tucci's wisdom. She noticed Cosmo and Frank sitting next to each other without their usual antagonism, with guards down, not up. Isabella seemed to tie Donna and Angie together, as if erasing the line between them.

Silvia's main concern was Frank's frequent gazes at Donna from across the table. Maybe he was admiring how pretty she looked with her beet red lipstick and elegant black, sleeveless dress. Maybe he was hoping that she had changed her mind about him. Her other main concern was with Vince and Doug, but Doug wasted no time in spurring up a conversation about Berkeley, allowing her anxiety about them to subside. It turned out that Doug had lived close by Berkeley for a short while. Of course, it was in some place in Silicon Valley, a place that Vince would probably never set foot because it was too conservative. None-the-less, Doug knew about the general area.

"You're gonna love it out there," said Doug, stretching his arms out over his tired looking face and perfectly styled hair.

"Yeah," said Vince, his tone of voice with a mixture of enthusiasm and cautiousness. "I'm a bit nervous about going so far away, but I think I'll like Berkeley."

"He's going to fit right in," added Silvia, making her big smile even bigger.

She assumed that Frank must have told Vince that he would be helping him with his tuition. Of course, there was always the chance that he would change his mind, maybe forty or fifty times more before Vince was safely out of the house. Silvia then thought of something she could do to prevent this from happening.

"Hey everyone," she said, standing up and banging a spoon on her water glass. She had never done anything like this and kind of surprised herself when she stood up to take center stage. If she had been more sophisticated, she may have waited to make her announcement when there was wine, thereby making it a toast.

"I just wanted to thank everyone for coming to celebrate Vince's graduation from high school and his acceptance into Berkeley, where he'll be going in the fall." Everyone smiled at Vince and at Silvia, who then turned towards Frank and said, "And I would especially like to thank you, Dad, for making Vince's dream a reality. And also for making this gathering a possibility." And at this, everyone clapped their hands, especially little Isabella who saw this as an opportunity to clap and bounce and say "Yay!" in her baby voice. Frank had such a look of gratitude in his eyes, as though this moment, in itself, would be enough for him to live on for the rest of his life. She then sat down, Frank still smiling at her like she was the greatest person alive. She may have even been promoted to Frank's number one child that night.

From where Silvia sat, she could overhear fragments of all the conversations surrounding her. Donna was talking baby talk to Isabella, with Angie chiming in about her daughter's likes and dislikes. Cosmo was saying something to Frank about how his workplace was becoming less and less departmentalized, as more and more people were being laid off. Doug was still talking to Vince about the area in which he would soon reside. Everyone was interacting with each other, as if their fight-filled past had never existed, as if it had been completely erased from their minds. Maybe they *were* learning. Or maybe Grandma Tucci was sitting beside them all, silently showing them the way. Or maybe they were all just acting in accord to get through the night. Whatever the reason, it didn't matter. All that mattered was the absolute perfection of this time.

She felt a little covetous of this time, as she knew that, like all the really good things in life, it would pass too quickly. The thought of Frank's milkshake came into her head. She knew only too well that at any second Angie might remember how Cosmo rejected her offer to be Isabella's godfather. Or Donna might remember one of the many times Frank stumbled in from a night of drinking and cheating. They might all collectively remember that they should not be getting along so well.

This time was to be treasured and surely it was destined to become one of those special memories that Silvia could always look back on. She wanted to keep this time with her always in the same way that she had kept Grandma Tucci with her. She wanted to carry it with her for the rest of her life and throw away all of the bad family stuff that had lived within her for so long. She wanted this memory to be tattooed in her mind so that when things, once again, turned bad within her family, she would have this moment of light to hang onto.

Just as Silvia was enjoying the feeling of being so light that she felt as if she was floating over the table and watching everyone from above, the waiter came to the table with antipasto. Had it not been for the big gaping hole in her stomach, she would have floated a little longer. But she knew she needed to get some salad before her family finished it up. In fact, she knew to serve herself first, so that she could be assured of getting the best of what was in the bowl.

"You're taking all the tomatoes," said Donna to Silvia.

"I barely ate all day," said Silvia. "Give me a break."

Isabella began to make sounds and point to the bowl of lettuce as if she was trying to say "salad."

"She loves anything green," said her mother proudly. "You should see how excited she gets when I make spinach."

After bragging about her little girl, Angie jumped up and ran over to the waiter, smart phone in hand, to ask him if he could take a picture of all of them. Silvia couldn't believe that she had forgotten about getting a picture of the occasion. She was grateful that Angie had remembered and really grateful that Angie then said that she would email a copy to everyone.

Voices seemed to rise and fall together making a symphony of chatter. Around midway through dinner, Vince turned to Silvia and said, "Thanks for everything, Silvie." And she knew exactly what he meant by "everything," as if they had communicated telepathically. It wasn't just making this celebration happen. It wasn't just announcing to everyone that Frank would be helping him with his tuition, thereby, making sure Frank abides by the promise he had made and broken several times. It was for all that she had taught him this past month, like getting along with people who had different values than him, biting his tongue and being diplomatic, remembering the good in all people, and being able to forgive.

Donna seemed oblivious to the awkwardness present between Cosmo and Angie, as she was too preoccupied with feeding her grand-daughter. But Silvia was perfectly aware of it. She was relieved when Cosmo made the opening gesture towards Angie. What he said was nothing like a piece of ordinary conversation. It was nothing like, "So how's North Jersey?" or "Do you make it in to New York a lot?" or "You must be enjoying being a mom, huh?" Anything like that would have been too banal for Cosmo. Instead he grabbed something from his pants pocket and said playfully, "I gotta magic trick for Isabella." He walked over to his niece smiling his big, goofy smile, while Angie followed with her eyes. He acted like a big clown and looked like one, even without face makeup and big floppy shoes. Isabella looked at him as if she knew she was about to be entertained.

"Oh look! You have something behind your ear," said Cosmo to the little girl, as he put his hand behind her ear and pulled out a quarter. She began to laugh and jump up and down in her high chair.

When he took his seat again, grinning big and wide, Angie patted him on the shoulder affectionately and said, "I didn't know we had a magician in the family."

"Yeah," he responded. "I guess I should be learning some more tricks now that there's a little one around."

Silvia was so touched by the whole exchange and she thanked her big brother with smiling eyes. He reciprocated her graciousness by saying the very thing that she had wanted to hear him say for the past month. She just wished that he had not said it from across the table so that everyone could hear.

"I have been giving that Portland thing some more thought. It does look like a great place. Maybe I will come out there with you and check it out."

She stared back at him with bewilderment. She was happy to hear this, but not overjoyed. She told him that she wasn't sure that she would be going any time soon but that it might be a great thing for the two of them to move there together one day. For the first time in a very long time, there was no rush to get to some place new. She didn't need to continue to search for the perfect place. She felt that she had found it right where she was. She felt that it would come with her wherever she went, whether that place was Portland, New Jersey or on the moon.

The magic continued throughout the delicious dinner that included homemade raviolis, chicken cacciatore, and spaghetti with clams. The laughter and the conversation blurred together into one big, gorgeous thing. Through Silvia's hard work, the circle of fighting that went on and on, in their family and the families that preceded them, had been broken. Most likely it would be temporary, as someone would inevitably remember something to be angry about. But she didn't have the future and she didn't have the past. She only had now and now was good.

It wasn't until they had all started to walk out to the parking lot that Silvia remembered the painting. "I have something to show you all," she said, leading them over to her car. She opened her trunk and took out the painting. At first, all of their voices simultaneously declared what a great painting it was. Then Angie squabbled a bit about how she didn't like the eyes that her sister had given her. And Cosmo said that she made him too lanky. Frank said that he was much better looking in real life than in the painting. Vince and Donna just stood there admiring this thing of beauty. And then a great silence overtook them all, and their voices melted in the air. It was the kind of silence that was bigger than any sounds that could be heard. It was the same sound that Silvia had heard in the Cape May sunset. It was the sound of togetherness. The sound of six becoming one. The sound that rises above it all. The sound of peace.

THE END

Acknowledgements

James "Gaddy" Gadbois
Annamae Jacobs
Charlotte Sanders
Bob Finlayson
Linda Watson
Alicia Young